My Coney Island Baby

My Coney Island Baby

Billy O'Callaghan

JONATHAN CAPE
LONDON

1 3 5 7 9 10 8 6 4 2

Jonathan Cape, an imprint of Vintage,
20 Vauxhall Bridge Road,
London SW1V 2SA

Jonathan Cape is part of the Penguin Random House group of
companies whose addresses can be found at
global.penguinrandomhouse.com.

First published by Jonathan Cape in 2019

penguin.co.uk/vintage

A CIP catalogue record for this book is
available from the British Library

ISBN 9781787330917
TPB ISBN 9781787331341

Typeset in 11.5/16 pt Stempel Garamond
by Integra Software Services Pvt. Ltd, Pondicherry

Printed and bound by Clays Ltd, Elcograf S.p.A.

Penguin Random House is committed to a sustainable future for
our business, our readers and our planet. This book is made
from Forest Stewardship Council® certified paper.

For Richard, my little brother,
a part of this story, and a part of us, still

I

The Boardwalk

The air out here is mean with cold. It was bitter on the journey out from Manhattan too, but nothing like this. This is bleakness without respite. An hour in the subway was an hour shielded from the wind, and now it is almost noon and already threatening snow.

Michael and Caitlin walk quickly, side by side, heads lowered, shoulders hunched. Apart from a couple of drunks in a doorway arguing mutedly over a bottle, and further out past Nathan's along Surf Avenue an elderly black man leashed by a length of orange clothes line twine to a ridiculously small dog, the streets feel deserted, locked down. Most of the stores along here are shuttered too, some closed for the season, others having already written off the day as a bad debt. Passing trade is below freezing. The few places that insist on remaining open – a liquor store, a 7-Eleven, some sort of a goodwill shop with stacks of used, spine-cracked paperbacks in wicker baskets still out on the window ledges and green plastic sacks of clothes lining the pavement – do so more out of stubbornness than duty. Apart from the 7-Eleven, which probably feels contractually obliged, these stores don't bother to burn much light. This afternoon, Coney Island feels like the end of the world, the last bastion just short of some great abyss, a place for the damned to drift, waiting their turn at nothingness.

They keep, as much as possible, to the shelter of the buildings. Words come in clenches, whistling and operatic, but it hurts just to breathe, and talking feels even worse. Caitlin holds her coat bunched closed across her throat in one fist. The wind is strong enough to pull tears from her eyes. It gusts and swirls around them, tugging at the hem of her overcoat, and she is glad that she thought to wear a scarf today, though she could have done with gloves, too. Her pockets are deep but provide barely the suggestion of heat.

Snow is forecast, torrents of the stuff, blizzards, but for now it is holding back, except for the occasional spatters that hit like thrown stones and leave imagined bruises in the air and on the skin. The sky above is mud, a bullying slob of grey running into grey, slaughtering detail and definition. Caitlin leans into Michael and they press on at a staggering half-run. Because there is nothing else to do, now that they have started in this direction.

This is the worst stretch of road, just here, where they hurry out across the empty street, because it takes them headlong into the mouth of the gale. They are forced to walk almost in one another's arms and the noise of the wind howling in their ears drowns out even the shambles of their own laboured breathing. And when, finally, they leave the promenade and turn out onto the pier the wind lifts to new intent and tears at them, at their faces and their clothes, turning them dishevelled in a hurry. All they can do is make for the line of shacks, the boardwalk stalls locked down and abandoned for the season. Shelter to press against, and a hiding place.

'Christ,' Caitlin gasps, then laughs with a kind of terror. 'It's like something out of Revelation.'

Startled by how close she has come to the run of his own mind, Michael takes hold of her, with one arm drawing her to his body. Needing her that close. She looks up at him. Her face has turned the colour of flour. A new depth of pale. She is wearing a subtle daub of lip gloss, a sanguine red already hours worn, but her mouth is small, pinched tight against the cold, and the definition counts for very little, even when she smiles. He thinks of geisha women; sweet, delicate dolls in sky-blue kimonos, with their faces blanched by powder and a tiny rosebud pout painted into place. Made to look girlish and demure but in possession of a secret fire somewhere underneath or deep inside, the kind of raging, ravishing inferno that in a single blast can smelt bone down to dribbling soup. Caught in Caitlin's wide, frightened animal eyes, transfixed by her drained expression, he glimpses, briefly and for the first time today, the merest hint as to who she truly is, or might be, or who she could be. She is a woman born to deceive, he suddenly realises. An angelic outer skin belying fiery lies within. And this is one of the details he loves most about her.

'The end won't be like this,' he says, his mouth close enough to taste her breath, and for her to taste his. 'When that comes we won't even know it. We'll be here, and

3

then a millionth of a second later, we won't be. Not even the dust of us.'

'Are you drunk?' she asks.

He shakes his head, and smiles. 'I'm too happy to be drunk.'

'Happy?'

'Of course. Hard to believe, I know, but that's how I feel. Because look where we are. Look who I'm with.'

She sets a hand on his chest, bats him playfully. He closes the gap between them and kisses her. They take turns leading the way, since there is no one around to see. She finds his tongue and rolls it gently with the tip of her own, forces its pulp against the rim of her upper front teeth. He goes willingly. Her mouth has the heat of tea. She breathes into him and he breathes back. It is the perfect give and take, like waves, a kind of essence of sex. After a time, they ease apart, she instigating the break with a subtle bringing together of her lips. But the split is merely temporary, and designed simply to let her settle more comfortably against him. He leans back against a boarded-over stall, a long narrow shed painted in faded laurel-green emulsion, heavy-duty stuff that, even so, has weathered badly, and she folds herself again into his embrace. When one hand slips downwards and cups the demure swell of her ass he feels her mouth bend into a grin, forcing his own to follow towards laughter, and when they close their eyes, they are children, playing at being in love. By making a nest just beneath the skin, certain memories put themselves beyond the reach of change.

*

4

Below and on their left, the white strand stretches emptily northwards, acting like a framing edge to the main event, the bigger picture, the enormous sprawl of ocean that, in close, bucks and moils. Frothing, needlepoint flecks mottle a surface dull as lead, great furred bilges of surf break hard against the shoreline. Further out, a peculiar sense of calm prevails, at least to the eye, some fast shuffling deception of distance coupled with the perpetual twilight's condensed striations.

Pressed together, they listen, with delicious and undisclosed terror, to the crashing sounds of the water careening against the pier's stanchion posts and to the wild, mournful bleating of the wind.

'Barb's got cancer,' Michael says, speaking the words in a soft, almost absent fashion.

For an instant, she is sure that she must have misheard, yet there is a sense of the news in his demeanour. She searches his face, but he is staring out over her shoulder towards the horizon.

'What?'

'In the kidneys. It's been there for a while, but you know what she's like. She's the kind who has to piss black before a bell goes off.'

He winces and purses his lips, as if the words themselves hurt to speak.

'Jesus.'

The weakness of his expression strikes Caitlin all at once. His flesh has the bruised shade and texture of putty, and hangs from his strongest features, thickening his nose and lending a maudlin heft to his cheeks. His mouth seems to be receding too, sinking finally from the strain of

5

holding back years' worth of the things that so badly need saying. He has recently turned forty-eight years old. January sixth. Forty-eight is no age any more, not the way it once was, but lack of sleep, added to the many other extenuating factors, has caused rust to set in. Also, he is probably forty pounds overweight, and that, even on a thickset five-ten frame, is the sort of burden that takes a toll. There is a hint of lameness in his walk now, his joints answering to the first seasonal tweak of sciatica; his head hangs, and his big shoulders have lately taken on a certain constricting roundness. She knows what age can do, and how suddenly its effects can grab the light, but what makes it all so difficult to accept is that, in her mind, he remains so young, so vibrant, still the strong, loving man who first approached her in that bar all those years ago and who made her fall so hard. Decades ago, now. The arrangement they keep encourages delusion, of course, meeting as they do just once a month but every month, the first Tuesday without fail. With such a bulk of their lives spent in wait, reality has been allowed, even encouraged, to turn fragile.

When he can no longer comfortably evade her studied gaze he meets it and sighs, a heaving gust that sings of its weariness. And all at once, she recognises him. The way his eyes narrow and elongate, the paper-cut sharpness of his lips, the smile always apparently so little-meant once it breaks the surface but which feels precious as it wells. This is him. This is who he is: her big, lumbering Irishman. She leans in against his neck. The sigh is for her, she knows. Everything is for her. Shuddering loose from the grip of the world in order to free himself fully and completely, even if only for these few hours.

'So far, they've taken vats of blood and done a battery of scans. She's already had two biopsies, and now they want to take a look at her liver. She's under a Mr Wylie, who's supposed to be one of the top men in his field. He seems like a decent sort. At least, he looks you in the eye when he speaks to you, which is more than most of them will.'

Caitlin's heart is beating very hard, the pulse undulating upwards from her chest and flooding her mind, and for a moment she is uncertain about what to do, whether to pull away from the embrace or to wrap herself even more tightly to Michael's body. But the grip of his arm around the small of her back absolves her of choice, and so she presses her face into the pocket of his neck again, closing her eyes, as if this alone will be enough to shut out the world and keep her safe. Her throat has also tightened, and words feel impossible as anything other than whispers.

'Jesus,' she repeats. 'That's such awful news. I'm sorry.'

'I know,' he says. 'I know you're sorry. I'm sorry, too. But it's not enough. Wylie is doing what he can, but the prognosis isn't great. I think he fears the worst. Surgery was initially mentioned, but the tests revealed more than he'd have liked. He hasn't said anything outright, but he keeps dropping words like "aggressive" and "metastasis" into his sentences, words that don't exactly fill you with confidence. And it's only going to get worse from here. Barb is scheduled for fifty-five cycles of chemotherapy, and that will be an entirely new kind of terrible. She'll almost certainly lose her hair and we've been told to expect heavy bouts of nausea and fatigue. I've read about it. The chemo hits everything, good cells as well as bad. That's how it works. It's poison to the system, which to me makes no sense whatsoever. For now she's coping, but that's mostly still the shock, I think.'

The words pour from him without inflection, and his stare has knitted itself to some far-off place or thing, the dreamy trance of a boxer who has been knocked half a dozen times too many in the head, or of a drunk who has abandoned all pretence of being otherwise. Then his hand climbs her spine and gently cups the back of her head, and his mouth, high above her ear, makes the sound of a kiss. The wind is everywhere, immense. Even the locked-down shack behind them groans and rocks. She tightens her embrace, fastening herself to him. His arms squeeze around her in response.

'I'm to blame. Wylie told us that the cancer has been active for upwards of a year. That's how he put it. And he looked at me when he spoke. As usual, Barb had done a decent job of hiding it, but after all the years we've been together, you'd think I'd be able to read her. I should have picked up on the signs. Because they were all there. Some nights I'd wake and find her gone from the bed, and she's lost so much weight these past few months that she can't even sit comfortably any more. Her bones have started to show.'

Back when he and Caitlin had first started going together, he'd been keeping down a second job, weekend shifts, in a garage owned by Barbara's cousin, Jerry. His main work, then as now, was in sales, the sort of number that passed in most minds for smart because it kept you in a chair most of the day and made a suit compulsory, part of the uniform. But the weekend work answered a different need.

This was dogsbody stuff, the slog of lumps and grinds, him being next to useless when it came to anything engine-related but able enough across the shoulders and willing both in body and in mind to sweat. He was paid, of course, folding cash too, twenty-five or fifty a day, or however much passed for fair to middling back then. But he'd not really gotten into it for the money.

Even beyond the duties of familial loyalty, Jerry was a decent type, and badly in need of help. The man wasn't slacking; he worked long hours and put in genuine shifts but he was the kind who needed someone in it with him, a commiserating hand when panic hit and everything turned cluttered. For him, the books were just too much, and business simply wasn't his thing. The solution to that would turn out, eventually, to be Wanda, a woman with thirty square in the sights of both barrels but who had never quite shaken off the girlish part of herself. She was tall and thin, wiry, with the kind of svelte, rippled body that any dancer, Broadway or exotic, would have gone into serious hock in order to possess. She chewed gum, kept her rust-coloured hair in a thick permanent and wore short shorts or mini-skirts, alternating back and forth between vinyl black and the lustiest scarlet, every day of the year apart from Christmas. She talked baseball like she had shares in the game and knew some diamond cuss-words. And, because there are all kinds of excuses for love, she was a veritable sweetheart about anything to do with Jerry. Beyond capable in every direction worth taking, she stepped in, seized control of the receipts, logged the inventory, fixed book-ings, handled orders and bills, and was single-handedly responsible for organising him into someone even halfway

9

successful, as a man as well as a mechanic. She also slept with him, cooked and cleaned for him, washed his clothes and, eventually, married him. But at the point where Jerry first began to slip into meltdown mode, she was still a good year off in the future, and so the onus of keeping cousin-in-law upright and afloat fell from a height on Michael.

The situation was quickly deteriorating. Jerry had taken over the garage, against all perceived wisdom and on the back of a pretty nihilistic mortgage, some eighteen months previously, and for a while he'd gotten by on credit and sheer enthusiasm. Starting up in trade is beastly without backing cash, so credit was the only option: credit on materials, credit on wages, credit on the jars of instant coffee and the pre-packaged Twinkies that he slurped and ate standing hunched beneath some gaping hood in an effort to save time and money on lunch breaks. Credit which, in the long run, only made everything immeasurably worse. And once the magnitude of the accrued debt exposed itself, he got to drinking all ends up, the sort of brown-paper-bag stuff that requires both hands free just to keep pace, and in whiskey or whatever he had a fuming temper that would snap like rotten twigs at the least provocation. After those around him had bailed in search of better cover, what he needed, especially at weekends, was someone who knew him and could tolerate his ways, preferably someone who could also crank a jack, change a tyre and hoist a winch without needing to be screamed at and watched over, and who could refrain from going all Joe Hill on him about lunch breaks, toilet breaks, smoking breaks, time-and-a-half after six, double hours Sunday.

Michael provided a willing solution.

Six months on from the burial of what would prove to be their only child – their little boy, James Matthew – the world of things had changed. A few seconds of joy and then fourteen weeks, two days and five hours of waiting for the kind of inevitable end that still, even months later, even years, packed all the devastation of a train wreck. Everyone copes differently with that sort of ordeal. Some turn to prayer, others to therapy. Michael's way was to peel back from Barb's clinging and tuck himself into some muscle work. He felt bad about doing it, but then he felt bad about so many things that after a few weeks it became just another entry on his list of shame. What he needed was to work bodily and hard, and at the garage there were no boundaries. He could sweat himself almost to the point of blackout, could go at it until his arms ached and his back felt set to snap, and then he could keep on, wallowing in that pain, wanting to hurt in all the ways that he could actually understand. It was physical and masculine, and in its way redemptive. And later, after they'd crawled out into the darkness and bolted up the doors on another good Sunday, he and Jerry would hit a bar, some joint that had a game going on a small screen or, depending on their mood, somewhere with low lights and piped jazz, the kind of blue notes that you can only really get in back-alley places and unlicensed cellar bars, those holes in the night that call to mind the speakeasy atmosphere of a time when booze played by different rules. A pealing trumpet, an alto sax that squeals its way into that pocket beyond tears, in where grief has four solid walls, a ceiling and a floor, and where the sound can build and swell and bounce.

It was in one of these places that he first caught sight of Caitlin. She was a kid then, twenty-two, but possessed of a freshness that had long since faded from his life. Already married but somehow still girlish, still apparently light with curiosity as to the limits of the world, and soft all the way through. The yellow and puce flower patterns of her summer dress must have been entirely unsuited to the autumnal blow, but for a barroom its cut was perfect, the cheap cotton cut clinging to her hips, waist and breasts in a way that emphasised delicacy, and cupping her ass like grabbing hands when she picked up her drinks from the counter and walked back across the floor to the booth in which her friend Sally sat idling with a green plastic throwaway lighter. She'd ordered a Sea Breeze and a Mojito, clearly not their first of the evening judging by the way she smiled when she caught him watching her from his place at the bar. Head a little down but eyes big and all the way up, acting coy only as a tease. An hour or so later, when she approached the bar again, he was by then far enough along on beer and shots to slip down off his barstool, move casually alongside her and ask if she would allow him to buy her a drink. Even now, he can recall the wide-open silver of her eyes, a shade like ocean water on a white day. Her skin seemed to gleam even in the bar's dim light, and her mouth held back as much as it could, keeping close-lipped against a smile until something caused her to give up. No memory survives of how she replied to his advance, or even what magic words of his made her decide that he was worth a shot, but the image of her face as it was that evening, that Sunday night, remains burned

12

in sharp edges in his mind. When she spoke, she did so in a voice low enough to steam, and as Coltrane or Parker or Ornette Coleman or whoever it was dragged soul and then spirit squealing across the barroom ceiling, he could do nothing but lean in to catch what she was offering, to hear her words and breathe of her.

And on towards midnight, after enough of the corners had been taken off and enough waiting had been done, they settled for a dance, there on the barroom floor. They stood in one another's arms, dancing but barely moving, or moving like cobweb on a breath of night breeze, as tunes seeped one into the next. The skin of her temple pressed hot and damp against his cheek, and he bowed his head and told her things in murmurs that he had never shared with anyone else. Together, they felt complete. It wasn't about sparks. This was fusion, nothing less. And soon after, when it came time for them to part, he scribbled down his office telephone number and asked her to please call him, tomorrow, tomorrow morning if she could. She said nothing, just read the number with concentration, then folded the scrap of paper in two and then in two again and slipped it into the change pocket of her purse. They kissed once, a brief and almost cursory coming together of their mouths, and then she nodded goodbye, slipped from his grasp and hurried to join her friend across the barroom floor. He stood where she had left him and watched her climb the open side-wall staircase to the street above without once looking back, certain that he'd neither see nor hear from her again. In that moment, something shifted inside of him, a churning terror at the prospect of being forced to live his life apart from her. Ridiculous, considering they'd only just met, but nonetheless truthful.

'Talk about something else,' Caitlin says now, in a whisper. 'Please.'

'Like what?'

'Anything. Tell me about work.'

'Work?'

Michael tastes the word before catching the drift of its actual meaning. Work is a safe option, like the weather, or politics, or whatever is going on with the economy; discussable fodder with the skeletal tract left neatly and reassuringly in place. In your forties your sense of longing shifts, and pleases itself in comfort rather than thrills.

He smiles out of one corner of his mouth.

'Work is fine. The usual towers of paperwork, buyers who try to stiff-arm you come reorder time – the office full to popping with liars, back-stabbers and thieves. Nothing changes. We're hiring arch-criminals now, fresh from Ivy League borstals with their nose-flute accents and their grand-a-week coke habits. But they flap a Masters or a Doctoral certificate like it's the utmost guarantee of peace in our time, and use it as nothing less than a licence to pillage. Hardly ten minutes of my working day goes by now that I don't contemplate just damning the whole thing to hell and walking out while there's still a bit of life left in my carcass.'

'But you don't.'

He looks at her again, and shakes his head.

'No, I suppose I don't. Others can wake up one morning and just start running, clear across the world, some of them, like they're Gauguin or Brando or Marco fucking Polo. But that's a young man's game. When we're young and our horizons have yet to burn, we take risks that become impossible later on. Time makes us afraid. Maybe it's just that we pick up so many anchors along the way. I have dreams, just like everyone else, but when I was a kid, forty seemed old. Now I have fifty in my sights, and I'm feeling every minute of it. The truth is, I'm not a brave man. Stupid, maybe, but not brave.'

Caitlin slips from his arms and moves to his left side, and together they press their backs against the sheltering stalls and gaze out over the ocean. The horizon line has been rubbed away and there is nothing beyond the loose logic of suggestion to differentiate between water and sky. At a distance, everything seems soluble.

She reaches for his hand, clasps it in both of hers and then gently traces her fingertips over his knuckles. The bones at the back of his hand fan close to the surface and veins show in bluish twists through the opaque skin. It is the hand of an old man, its strength waning. Flecks of hair crawl from under the cuff of his shirtsleeve and spread outwards in a jagged splay, shadowy as spilt ink. Answering some subtle shift in her touch, he opens and spreads his fingers for her, inviting, urging. Then they stand a while, just gazing at the ocean, holding hands. She smiles, inwardly, and he catches a sense of it and they lean in close and kiss again. And this kiss counts for more than their first pass. It lasts for five or ten seconds, warm time made something else by shut-eyed darkness. Her lips part and a moment beats just a thrilling hesitation too long before she gets the flit of his tongue.

'Let's go to bed,' he says, dragging her body against his own again. He wonders if she can feel him through all the layers of clothes. He kisses her cheeks, slowly, and her eyes when she closes them. Her skin has an icy coldness from the lambasting wind, but she sighs with what feels like contentment, and he feels some of it, too. Out here, sheltering from a storm, it is almost possible to believe that the world has been made to exist entirely for their benefit, and that nothing else matters beyond their happiness.

'You've got a one-track mind,' she tells him. 'You know that?'

'I do,' he agrees. 'But it takes me where I want to go.'

'Big shot.'

'Biggest one in six counties.'

'Oh, and modest, too.'

'Naturally. And you know I'm only thinking of you, sweetheart. This is no kind of weather to be out walking. I'm just suggesting a way of generating some heat back into these old bones of ours.'

'Less of the old, if you don't mind.'

The hand against the small of her back drops a few inches and takes hold.

'You know the saying,' he says. 'The older the fiddle.'

'And you fancy yourself as a bit of a player, is that it?'

'Well, I've had no complaints so far.'

She tilts her head to one side, pretending to give the matter due consideration, though of course there is really nothing to decide. He watches her, amused, and feels himself falling for her all over again. Her expression is that of a young woman, a thoroughgoing innocent. She touches one corner of her mouth in a thoughtful way, her

16

eyes roll a little, and in that instant he understands that time means nothing, that age means nothing.

'Bed.'

'Bed.'

Her laughter strikes sudden and demure, a little chirping cough that flares and is gone, but it leaves behind its shape, showing teeth and then a pinch of tongue. This is how they are. In that bar, all those years ago, with jazz weeping from the speakers, they'd danced in no less but no greater a way than this. Out here, the air around them provides movement enough, and the song of the wind sluicing through the latticework of the pier is all the jazz they need.

'Let's finish our walk first,' she says, pulling away from him but keeping hold of his hand. 'Then we can talk about what comes after.'

Every stall and pitch is shut down, but it's a sad fact of life that, even during high season, this place only ever runs at half-speed any more. Half-speed at best. Because Coney Island feels done for. A rot has set in. And yet, being out here on a day like this still feels good. So fit for broken things, it has become their place. The best may be lost but an air of romance remains, and settling is a matter of choice. They like it out here because it is far enough removed from where they are supposed to be. Out here, free of Manhattan's vast claustrophobia, there is still sky to be had.

And even on such empty afternoons as these, so torn asunder by winds blowing muddy with the threat of snow, memories of how the boardwalk was in better times feel barely a breath away. Days when, come March or April and clean on through the searing, sultry doo-wop months of summer to the very marrow of late October, the hot-dog stands and the ice-cream vendors turned a roaring trade, when for a nickel or a dime and right before your awestruck and disbelieving eyes, sackloads of sugar were spun into great mystical cotton-candy beards, when fire-eating unicyclists knife-juggled their way through acts of uncountable daring, when the timbers shook and thundered beneath your feet, rattling under the strain of stampeding kids, and the ringing bells of the one-armed bandits struck lucky all around. The air smelled sweet and salty then, the waves came and food was fried, and everything, everything, was noise, a wall of sound, sheer and unabated. The thrilled screams as teenage boys rough-housed with and manhandled their bikini-clad girls, the accordion wails of the buskers, the hip strains of the latest hit number leaking from a dozen boom-boxes all tuned to the same station, and now and again the stabbing thrusts of some nearby ride's wildly spinning calliope song. All were mere ingredients in the melding cacophony of a hundred simultaneous rackets eager for their piece of day.

And even on a noon so crushed by wind as this, being out here is still worth anything for the way in which it indulges their particular strain of make-believe. The stalls are closed, padlocked, but it is easy for Caitlin to convince herself that they are not actually abandoned at all; they have merely settled into a comfortable wintry hibernation. And the same can be said, and imagined, of the men who work these stalls, the fast-talking types who grin like crooks out of sheer job satisfaction but at least as much because it gives them the opportunity to boast of their missing teeth, or their golden replacements. Men who in different eras would have plied the trade of pirates, who wear T-shirts sweat-stained into an entirely different range of colours above and far beyond the call of their natural dutiful shade and who have too much hair in the wrong places and too little in the right. They are missing now, she tells herself, purely because they acknowledge the rules of seasonal employment, and have no doubt returned to the murk of the city in order to eke their way through these grim months, spending their time hunched above a jack-hammer or tucked into a short-order apron, or even, God forbid, a salesman's suit. But they are brave, despite appearances, and wise too, because they understand the truth of things. They have the hearts of sea dogs but the keenness of explorers, and salt as well as fat courses through their veins. They can endure, and so they brace themselves and do what needs doing, the digging, the flipping, the flogging, because they know that daytime always follows night and that, soon enough, fortune will again smile on them and send them scuttling back here, armed with all manner of sugar, grease and questionable meat, to bask once more in the summery splendour of some truly lovely boardwalk living.

Gleams of pleasure can be had even from those times rightfully owed to sadness. It is simply a matter of sifting for gold, and the passage of time grants wisdom of a kind. Buddhists strive to live like that, keeping strictly within the moment. Caitlin knows that the day ahead holds darkness, and there are matters which need discussing and which will likely see all of this brought to its dreaded brink, but for now she can smile, and mean it. Since the night she and Michael danced their way into one another's lives, a shared day has never passed without her feeling at least a few seconds' worth of overwhelming joy. Such moments might occur during sex, but the feeling has never been exclusive to that, and often simply walking hand in hand can be enough, or having her name spoken by him in that certain kind of breathless way. When guilt or doubt gets in, she cries, without hesitation and denying herself nothing, because these hours are so limited. In this manner, negativity is washed away even as it emerges, and the tears become something separate from herself. She has learned that it is possible to cry and still feel good. Such a sensation, she is sure, can only come from love, and every detail of theirs is intensified in its distillation.

She no longer questions her feelings. If she feels like smiling, she smiles. You learn to make the best of any situation, or else there is only death. The news about Barbara is terrible. Caitlin has seen cancer up close, having at nineteen years old been forced to watch it pick away layers of her mother, until what remained was a piece of meat living out its last, a body beyond the comprehension of anything except pain. These past two and a half decades, give or take, Barb has existed along the periphery of her affair with Michael, a ghostly presence, tall and slim and statuesque, immaculately hewn yet blanketed in some eternal melancholy. Beautiful, if beauty is strict in limiting itself to chiselled and Romanesque, but never less than pretty to any eye, her corn-coloured hair worn forever short and full, running a gamut of perms, bobs, bell-cuts and pageboy looks, always obliviously underlining some definition of stylish. But associations have the effect of whittling away reality. When Caitlin thinks of Barbara now, her mind dredges up the image of a cramped hospital room, just like the one that had housed her mother, a small box of space lit by nothing but hallway leakage and reeking of an antiseptic designed to mask something immeasurably worse. Flowers in an opaque glass vase, their vivid colours dimmed but a well-meant gesture good to the eye from a yard or more away, conning with the illusion of life thanks to some water and a little chemical encouragement. And in the bed alongside, slumbering beneath ten ebony inches of wall-mounted crucifix, a body withered nearly to dust, a face recognisable from every angle as nothing less than the face of cancer, and turning human again only when daylight waxed or when those big sad molasses eyes fluttered momentarily open.

Braving the wind, they push on, out towards the end of the pier. Michael keeps his teeth clenched and bared, his gaze fixed to a point fifty or one hundred yards ahead, as if this will somehow help them to their destination. When they do reach the end, the protective railing holds them back, a barrier in advance of the abyss, because Coney Island is today a precipice. Years and decades have layered the timber with a rind of mucus, the ghoulish algae-tinge of ocean and ocean breath. And beyond is where the Titans dwell, Caitlin thinks, feeling for the half-remembered lessons she learned in school. Myth, of

21

course, but myth is only so until proven real, and belief is really just a question of awareness, of knowing where to set the line between the stubborn absolutes of fantasy and truth. And watching how the ocean comes and goes, thickening, churning, always alive, always breathing, bullying and pressing the shoreline and then abating in order to gather again ahead of the next onslaught, she thinks about the Titans and imagines a casual gaze passing right over them, either by accident or out of ignorance misreading their features and expressions as nothing but tide, the long scan of waves, water glassed with light and reflected sky, failing to recognise exactly who or what the hell they are.

'Are you dreaming?' Michael asks.

She glances up at him, wanting to catch some keenness in his expression. But she has misread his interest. His eyes continue to search over the realms of ocean. In the distant east, the water looks like sheets of corrugate, the ridges shining dull as tarnished steel, the troughs thick with shadow.

'I think I am,' she murmurs in reply.

'Of us?'

She hesitates. 'Of us, and other things.'

Something in his face shifts. Concentrated mainly in the flesh bagging around and beneath his narrowed eyes, in different light it could almost be a wince. But these gales make serenity difficult.

'I suppose I can live with that,' he says. 'As long as I'm somewhere in the mix.'

'You are,' she assures him, but she looks away to keep from having to talk about what most needs saying. The

22

end times have never felt closer than now but, with these few hours available to them, there'll be time enough for the hard words and the different flavours of goodbye.

Luxuriating in the spray that dusts their faces, they look out across the plain of water that stretches to the horizon and all the way beyond. So many thousands of surface miles cloaking uncountable leagues of depth. And such secrets. This ocean has an aspect of space, in that a vast acreage of what lies beneath is mere theory. There because it must be there, as God is, for believers. Or the Devil, or the perfect note, or the man in the moon. Or the air. All that's needed is a leap of faith. Science and myth differ in scores of wild, ferocious ways, but have at least this in common. And six feet under, down where the day's light can no longer penetrate and where even the strongest winds fail to reach, lies a whole other existence, running to a perfectly ordered cycle of feeding, multiplying and dying. Getting on with things, but beating to an entirely different drum. Down there, right and wrong cease to exist, and the earth itself is the only god that counts, the only one capable of disturbing the accepted reverie.

Everything is changing. Too late, Barbara's cancer has invented possibilities. Beautiful women often age badly, and trying too hard somehow only quickens the rate of deterioration. For others, though, the problem is a surrender into neglect. Michael said once that it was losing the child which entrenched Barbara's isolation. Always with a tendency towards the fey, she was knocked a step out of time by James Matthew's death, and into some in-between state from which she'd never quite returned.

Even when you had her in a room you rarely had more than a piece of her. Knowing this, and accepting it as a certain truth, has for decades helped assuage their guilt. Because even if the cancer now should break her entirely down and twist her into something monstrous, it will probably only matter to the surface of who she is. Her depths, if Michael is correct, have already long since met with ruin.

Caitlin closes her eyes and wills herself down into that more controlled darkness. She feels for Michael's hand, and counts the seconds until his fingers close in answer around hers. She makes it to five, then ten, and when after ten there is still no touch a worm of dread stirs within her, awakening all manner of fears, all the things that have been there for a long time but increasingly so in recent times, things she hates even to contemplate. But then, just as she is about to open her eyes again, his hand finds hers. It squeezes, gently, and everything once more begins to settle. His skin against hers lends cool reassurance, and a pulse insinuates from somewhere very deep within.

They stand there then, holding hands and holding onto one another, fettered together by this single willing touch, each thinking the sort of thoughts that approach the same subject from different sides. His coat's hem flaps madly, and even though he is keeping her mostly sheltered, the skirt of her dress catches a sudden sweep of wind and billows, and all she can do is wrestle it back against her legs, gather up the loosest flumes of the material and hold the hem snug against one thigh.

'All right,' she says, finally, acting all worn down. 'I give in. Time for bed.'

Michael puts his arm around her waist. She does not look at him and doesn't react when he kisses her cheek, high up, close to her eye. She wants to imagine that he is smiling, and that he is happy. They turn away from the vista of the ocean and the enormous clotted sky, and walk in a tight huddle once more down the pier, their backs braced against the day's vicious sweep.

II

Limbo

They'd just started in on their second year of marriage when Barb fell pregnant. Until then everything had been bliss. Michael was working at full tilt, the way you can when life still seems straightforward as typeset. Rabid for sales and all the good things that sales could bring, things like the cramped but lovely rented apartment in New Rochelle, the late-model Chevy Nova, clean and well enough maintained to pass as almost new, and the sort of cash flow, moderate but consistent, that kept bills to a bearable minimum.

The car was their biggest indulgence, a real financial drag, but because his job begged him frequently out of town it not only let him make the backwaters of Connecticut and Maine hauling the sort of samples that he could never have managed by bus, train or plane, it also offered the occasional option of driving all night to catch breakfast at home instead of bunking down alone in some dank nowhere motel. When he first started at Jefferson's, he'd tried making do with public transport, had suffered the wrenched neck and the stiff back of long, lonesome hours spent away from the comfort of his own bed. But once married, he and Barb agreed that the car was worth a little extra bust of the hump, the five or ten more hours a week put in at the office, coming in early or staying late, making calls, wading through reams of paperwork, trying to free up that critical fraction more selling time that would make all the difference. Having to bear the added workload was not easy, especially with a beautiful young wife waiting at home, but even after every sundry demand had been met, there was always still fire enough to burn beacons. Because he was twenty-three years old and built to go around.

They spent their first year of marriage mostly falling in and out of days. Life was difficult and euphoric, cluttered with work, with running, snatching at words, keeping a hard pace and existing each only for the other. And late on, squeezing beneath the sheets only to find that, actually, sleep was not even the second most pressing thought in their heads. So much seemed to exist for them at once, every detail felt heightened, every touch, every sound, smell and taste. The darkness acted like a poultice on the world, drawing flavour. And Barb had this way of smiling as she dozed, a little teasing smirk that had him a balloon simply begging for the quick, brutal jab of a pin. Lovely and sweet and full of the kind of rumbling laughter that works so well in any situation but really comes into its own once the lights have been doused. Year One made a tide of the details, and living was all about finding means and opportunity at every turn. Contacts, strategies, bargaining, deals taken to breaking point, all sorts of asses kissed, promising the moon and stars down out of the sky, numbers cracked and hammered to a decimal or two above absolute death, for goodwill's sake, for kindness and fair exchange and, more often than not, out of sheer, straightforward desperation. And in between, and all around, the snatched moments of a high; some breakfast game of footsie, lunches taken standing up, finger-licking dinners, and beer sipped from a shared bottle or can while sprawled all the way beat and three-quarters broken in front of some old late-showing movie, something to raise a few peals, Jimmy Stewart, say, or Cary Grant: suave, debonair, all conman's grins and ever so slightly up to no real good. Either that or else one of the tough guys, Bogart, Lee Marvin, Mitchum. John Wayne. That sort of tough. Not muscle-bound; assured. Men who could take a crowbar to the knees and still keep in step, still keep jiving. What mattered wasn't who or what they watched but the fact that they had a sofa, and beer – or wine if that was the sort of night they were trying – and one another. With the lights turned low, Barb liked to sit with her usually bare legs tucked up beneath her or else stretched out across his lap. He'd stare at the movie, playing her at her own game by feigning a lack of interest in anything but the story unfurling across the screen, until twenty minutes or half an hour in when, almost of their own accord, his hands would go to work, helpless for her calves, her feet and the bones of her ankles, and finally, unable to hold himself back, the rest of her.

And then, some fourteen months along, without thinking a thought in such a direction, big news came banging. What had previously seemed like the height of

29

happiness turned suddenly anaemic. This new state was one of pure exaltation, like feasting after a fast, like the first break of light after a lifetime spent suppressed. Pregnant. Even the word made them gasp. Michael and Barb passed joyous at a hard gallop and felt themselves bordering on ecstasy, neither one of them less so than the other. Everything bloomed. Everything.

The child was born in late November, the twenty-seventh, minutes after the thinnest of watery dawns had seeped into a heavyweight sky. A boy, James Matthew, five pounds, six ounces. The twenty-seventh was nineteen days short of full term, but that trifling prematurity felt like nothing more than a bookish aside and no one seemed unduly concerned. A boy, a son, a fraction shy in the bounce department perhaps but that, everyone said, was fully to be expected. And the time could easily be made up.

A light had gone on somewhere, a subtle burn that revealed whole previously unnoticed edges, that readjusted colours and let them impact anew. Michael could not stop smiling. After a while his face began to ache from it, and yet his expression didn't change, didn't want to change. He smiled, and shook his head a lot, purely at the wonder of it all. And shattered with relief, Barb smiled too. Perfect as coins in a well, she said, every heavy breath marinated in the kind of laughter that fulfils much the same duty as tears. Perfect, too, as rainbows and neck nibbles and the good sort of country music, before the fungus of plastic and big hats set in, and perfect as that cosy position that can sometimes be found when an embrace closes just right and truly fuses, stopping time.

Later, when all still seemed okay, absolutely normal, when Barb was released and allowed home to recuperate, they lay nights together in bed, the two of them counting away the minutes and hours until the time when they could reasonably return to the hospital and be again where they most needed to be. Life for them had simplified itself down to pacing the hallways or sitting beside the incubator, admiring and praying for and watching with wonder their little miracle made real, studying how his tiny fingers moved, how his lips twitched, the slow steady swell and plunge of his stomach, the curves and putty-coloured planes of his small, almost-still body encased in glass beneath the jaundiced light. In bed, attempting to compensate for their missing piece, they lay pressed to one another, but not moving, too comfortable to move, and too exhausted, and so instead of moving they sighed and smiled and whispered things, taking turns at swapping long lists of perfections that sounded good but which still fell light-aeons shy of the crystalline perfection they had, by fluke or alchemy, somehow forged.

Over the years, a regular day for Michael meant coercing contacts into parting with that dollar more than they ideally wanted to spend, but only that dollar, not the entire bank vault, resisting fast gold in favour of the steadier yields accumulated through a slow-bleed method. Such sweet-talked deals accounted for some decent business, and the closing of them brought their own thrills, their own satisfactions, yet he understood, even so, that this was still just work, not life, and that the truly precious aspects of the day lay in the quiet moments, while out driving, say, or taking on board a cup of strong morning coffee or lying awake in bed and drinking in the myriad beauties of his sleeping wife. When he had time to weigh the world and his place in it, and to contemplate and reflect. In those moments, he'd indulge more profound notions, such as whether or not existence had meaning, design, even destiny, or whether the universe amounted to merely the random chance of a turned card. It was all less about answers than about the simple flexing of his mind's muscles and his heart's yearning. Some people are born to practicality; others, the dreamers of this world, need that sense of awe the way plants need the nourishment of the sun. He'd roll these questions around, knock them back and forth, wallow in them and be happy.

The balance of work, love and dreaming had been easy to cultivate, but then, in the heave of a heart's single slamming, the capsize came. Words were made flesh and the whole game found new and intensified focus. All that counted was James Matthew. From the twenty-seventh onwards, the universe and everything in it tightened like a fist around Michael, from the instant of first cry distilling down to a central population of three as well as a few peripheral attendants. The world became a second-hand double bed in a cramped but decently positioned city apartment and a hospital's machine-cluttered, permanently twilit maternity ward incubation unit. The in-between – whatever might have existed between one place and the other: the miles of street, the crowded subway, the weather – was nothing more than empty space, a vacuum to be traversed at warp speed. In bed, in the darkness, he and Barbara whispered of their dreams, and by day they sat in terminal wait, hoping for the best and praying away the end.

And then, finally and probably inevitably, a moment came when their prayers skipped a beat, and that proved enough to tip asunder the delicate balance. Blame fatigue, blame complacency, blame some sentient wickedness getting kicks from doling out hope and then viciously snatching it away again. Toying with them, taking their prayers, spinning out the plot line of a joke that could only ever end badly, but leading them on and on and still on until there was not another step to take. By mid-March it was all over. Fourteen heady, upside-down weeks. Worse, in some ways, was the fact that they arrived into the hospital to the news. An hour or so later than usual, too, exhaustion having made them tardy, the tiny delicious comfort of an accidental lie-in, a blind slamming of the alarm for five minutes more, just five minutes that somehow became thirty, forty-five. They woke in panic, bypassed breakfast, dressed on the run and opted for the folly of the car instead of going the usual rush-hour subway route. Thinking that they could somehow reclaim the time lost, not understanding at all how these things actually worked. They came out the other end quivering with anger and fear but still utterly unprepared. An hour had made all the difference.

Suddenly, they were tumbling. And it was such a help-less, pathetic kind of fall.

'Move on,' people told them, once the immediate after-glow of grief began to bruise. People are conditioned to tolerate a certain amount, because they want, and try, to be understanding, to at least be seen to feel compassion and empathy. But this tolerance is not perpetual. A few days were fine, a week's worth, perhaps a little more, but anything too much longer than that began to press against a fairly uncompromising statute of limitation. The kindness offered was genuine but, as patience inevitably thinned, began to show strains of torpor. And everyone had a take on what had happened. Doctors, nurses, even relatives. All were careful to keep their tones demure and their expressions serious. But all, in their chosen way, pushed a pragmatic agenda. It happened, and yes, it was tragic, the very worst kind of sad, but it had not succeeded in stopping time. The world was still the world. The inference was clear: leave it as it lies and step away. Move on.

What they all said was what, in their minds, seemed like the best thing to say, but they could speak in such terms only because James Matthew was nothing to them, not really. A fleeting moment of grief, perhaps, but less for the actual living, breathing, flesh-and-blood, body-and-soul person than for the potential hinted at and then left so cruelly unfulfilled. They felt the loss, felt broken-hearted for it, but they didn't truly understand it because it did not impinge too directly on their own lives. They could still go home at night and close their eyes without having to take on the waiting torment of remembering the little boy inside that perspex glass-domed incubator, trapped tiny and yellow beneath a grilling light, yellow from a liver responding only to jump-starts, with a tube buried in his nose and more tubes running from the veins in both wrists and from strategic incision points in his stomach, chest and groin.

34

'Move on,' became the inferred mantra, repeated in a multitude of different words that all amounted to the same stock two-plus-two-equals solution, addressing Michael and Barbara not just while they were together and had one another to hold onto but also when they could be caught in separate states. Playing them each back and forth against the other and taking full advantage of their vulnerability and helplessness to ram the instruction home. And what the grieving couple were supposed to do, what was expected of them, was to nod and try to smile, even though they were both bleeding fountains inside. With the world on fire around them, their duty was to brace themselves against the pain and to whisper understanding. They were to lie, to themselves and to everyone else, and to keep at it until the lies became fact.

Those weeks immediately after the infant's passing could have represented a kind of beginning as well as an end, some transitory period between stages of life, natural progressions and all that bullshit. But instead of facing front and waging some sort of healing war, Barb and Michael, in abject fashion and with hardly a whimper, simply surrendered. They'd lost their fight, and were spent. And what followed was, in effect, dead time, just as much as the time that had immediately preceded it. Even more so, in fact, because that previous period, those months spent hunched on seat edges in a cramped and sterile hospital room, penned in from every angle by a necessary slew of flickering monitors and chirping machines, had at least indulged their delusions and let them believe in the notion if not the actuality of hope. And even later, after all such hope had faded, it still let them continue with the ruse and presented them with way after way of trying to comfort themselves and one another on lies that, yes, were sheer and unadulterated but which were also undeniably honourable. But this new emptiness offered nothing so supportive, not even the succour of an obvious falsehood. In the weeks immediately after their child's death, they found themselves cut loose to drift until they either happened their way to shore or else slipped under and were lost in the deluge.

One of the most difficult things to accept was just how literal the end had proven. A murmured apology, following on from the pulling of an actual physical plug. Christ. It was like switching off a light. That definitive. If pressed, Michael might have had to admit that, yes, it was final and at least to a certain extent clean, but there was still something too contrived about it, as if the hospital were acting on his decision, or his and Barb's, as if they, as distraught parents, had any kind of choice or input in the matter. What had happened was that, somewhere along the way, at some godforsaken hour during the smudge of weeks and months, he'd been taken aside and told that he needed to sign this form, this among all the others. It was nothing to get worked up about; a waiver, but a mere formality in cases such as this, because while the current numbers suggested with a ninety-nine per cent assurance that all would be fine, the very fact alone that there was even the most minuscule possibility of a slip meant the doctors had to keep themselves prepared and in a position to act, and act fast. Signing this form covered everyone and would allow them a free hand if something were to change between now and whenever. And, if such-and-such did happen, to do whatever was deemed medically necessary, to make the judgement call based on their combined decades of experience and expertise. They were talking about off-chances, of course, but were such a situation to occur then every second would have a numbered worth. A quick response was critical, and might prove the difference between miracle and tragedy. Michael had stared at the form and let the persuasions of the two doctors wash over him, but he could not bring himself to even think about understanding. All he could do, in the end, was sign. He sat in a leather-cushioned chair still warm from some recent occupancy, nodded his head and mumbled sounds from somewhere deep beneath his trance, and finally he took the offered pen and scrawled his name beside a tiny looped x. The doctors watched, leaning in on either side, one of them – the older of the two – pointing out with a long thin index finger where a set of initials was also required and where a box needed ticking. Neither had cared to inform him that what he was doing, essentially, was signing the death warrant on his only son.

Nobody wants a child to suffer, just as nobody wants a child to die. But how far can the limits be pushed before the definitions of ethics and morality turn reprehensible? The answer presented to Michael and Barbara, in a voice without edges, felt like a clawing interpretation. When nothing works except by machine, when even the most outlandish medical possibilities of recovery have been explored and exhausted, when finality offers the only definitive way of alleviating unbearable pain and the only humane option left available is to let the body run itself down. Floating in low sound just above a whisper, tenuous around the certainty of its facts, it was an answer, but one that failed to address how a person was expected to deal with the actual instant of end. How long would it take to realise that the heart was done, and how were you supposed to make sense of that? Because, even within the roll of the final beat, the nothingness of death must have felt impossible. For such a thing as life to exist and then, within a finger-snap, to see it snatched away, seemed not only bad magic but something infinitely worse because where even the darkest sorcery was concerned nothing had to be permanent. Everyone had words to say, advice to offer, assurances to make, but how could they even begin to know what it was like unless they'd been cornea-close, until they'd felt the stone-and-dirt stench of another's last few breaths against their lips and tongue? There are no words for something like that, and surely nothing for a soul to do, in the moment and even in the aftermath moments, but to stand there and try not to wince, try not to fucking scream.

Back when he was a boy, seven or eight years old, Michael had the opportunity to watch glass being blown. An uncle of his father's worked for Waterford Crystal and, giving assurances that it was something genuinely worth seeing, made arrangements for him to visit the factory. Michael was excited at the thought of escaping Inishbofin, taking the ferry across and then the long bus journey down across the country from Galway, having the opportunity to pass through cities and towns and getting to spend a night or two nights on another coast, in a strange house with people he knew only by blood.

38

He didn't question his good fortune, even though, to him, at that age, glass was just glass, a substance that seemed simply to exist, and without the least mystique. So he was completely unprepared for the actual facts of the process, the swelling and elongating of huge fiery bubbles, the sort of elastic flexing that challenged gravity and then in countless brazen ways defied it. That his mind should somehow equate such a day as that with a random later one spent standing in a hospital room, watching on through a wall of glass as his little baby boy worked so slowly and thoroughly towards a death most undeserved, seemed at surface level equal parts astonishing and incomprehensible. Watching, waiting for it, even from a particular point onwards ashamedly expecting it, yet still being rocked inside out by the impact, still feeling the savage, vacuous suck of its implosion, when the inevitable did finally pan out.

Logic seemed to play no obvious part in the association; rather, the whole thing had about it the sense of a gunshot fired blindly into the night, a bullet going from here to there, wherever here was, wherever there might be, vaguely directed but certainly nothing more solidly intended than that. Two thoughts, two experiences separated by a clutch of years and holding to polar opposite positions on the emotional spectrum, somehow fusing their way into cahoots by a spit of static, energising themselves into a kind of mutual being. Thinking about it, at the time and during the years that followed, trying to understand it from all manner of lateral perspectives, he identified within both moments an essential sense of shared awe, the same frozen, terrified wonder. Blowing glass was such a challenge to the belief system, the absurd captivation of watching a man breathe shapes out of a substance that appeared molecularly unmovable. Even to a mind as young as his it seemed to break definitive laws as to what qualified as truth. And then, following forward from this at a quantum stride of fifteen years, give or take, being forced to endure the hospital room situation that really was life, death and everything in between, and a particular but largely anonymous moment out of square thousands, hundreds of thousands, spent pressed to a sheet of glass which absolutely did not move, which wouldn't give so much as a millimetre of reassurance. That, perhaps, was the link, some cognisant flicker of subconscious past singing precisely the right note, the right song, the right lament, as his breath turned to fog before his eyes. And just beyond, in that space preserved for those hopeless cases who refuse to accept the facts of a summation, the tiny precious body of his little boy, James Matthew, naked and yellow-skinned and ribboned with tubes. Existing, though only just. That face, even tensed against the bursts of pain, that giveaway nose, Barbara's to a tee, those always lidded eyes and occasionally bobbing chin; and all flesh of Michael's flesh, or of theirs, his and Barb's combined, a miracle of their making, alive but untouchable, alive mainly because a machine said so and because a machine got to decide. And dead, in the end, for exactly those same reasons.

He had to ask where the hand of the Redeemer lay in all of this. He and Barbara had trusted, and obediently and in good faith let themselves be taken to some impossible height, hurrying blindly to a veritable pinnacle of contentment. And then, when they could not have been less prepared, came the edge, and beyond it, the fall, followed by an impact that shattered everything from the inside out. Was that the work of an Almighty? If so, then what separated deity from demon?

They'd had fourteen weeks as a family. Even with walls between them, the bonds were tied. And for most of that time, little changed. Day ran into day, and they sat and watched, waiting, concern kept in check only because the prognosis was always good and the reassurances came in soft smiles and with tidal regularity. Some days, a hint of hope, better numbers spilling from the monitors or the temperature holding steady by itself, but no obvious changes, nothing to break the wait. And living like that, at such a level of vigilance, tolled on body and soul in the same way that wind erases rock. Few lives are lived with such intensity of focus, and few can bear that for any significant stretch. For some, hours of it are too much. For Michael, and for Barbara too, it was weeks of positioning themselves day after day at the glass, sometimes in shifts but, more often than not, together. By the third month they'd gone beyond denial. The promises and insistences slowed and then fell away, leaving only dark thoughts to edge the silence. They kept to the glass only because there was nowhere else for them to be, and they watched until the sockets of their eyes throbbed and their minds, in a fluxing mess of guilt, relief, terror and the most bitter and deep-rooted form of grief imaginable, caught fire. Barbara often had to hurry away to the bathroom to be sick, and after a while they began to carry a hip-flask of whiskey with them, partly to deal with the nasty machine-made instant coffee and partly just so that they could feel some warmth inside themselves again.

The shifts, especially towards the end, brought on a kind of meditative visual hypnosis, repetitions without end of nothingness. This was the next realm after you passed from the state of helplessness into the forlorn place beyond. And as the last of the held-out hope began to splinter, Michael learned to live his life within the minutiae, bracing himself with each new breath the infant pulled in, certain on a level where nerves physically affect tissue that this inhalation was somehow definably different from the ones that had gone before and therefore must surely prove to be the last.

Part of the problem was how little the scene shifted. All they could do was hold themselves in a particular position, shoulders bunched, bodies stiff as boards in anticipation of some fall, some movement, anything at all beyond the scarce lag of a breath. Nothing else mattered, not work, not home, not the swarming Christmas city, the New Year city, the snow-flecked, frost-lacquered rooftops, the streets sluiced with gusting northerly winds. Standing there in that low-lit room, living from moment to moment, afraid to breathe themselves as everything deflated and stalled into stillness. And waiting out that stillness, churning with almost every mixed feeling it was possible to know, until finally the little fleshy shape before them began to bloat once more, the lungs heroically reinflating to begin the cycle all over again.

Barbara refused to give up. She made an addiction out of denial, taking to it the way a desert wanderer celebrates an oasis. When landed in battle, there are always some who turn and run and some whose only instinct is to dig in. James Matthew's status, which had, for what felt like the longest time, been supposedly secure, slowly about-faced and then flatlined to a whimper. The very doctors who'd earlier guaranteed so much and who'd hushed all hint of worry, now came, day on top of day, night into night, and spoke in muted tones, explaining how surprised they were that the situation had even managed to endure for so long. They stood and followed Michael's gaze through the glass and made it clear that while this continued display of struggle – or of courage, if you wanted to call it that – was in many respects admirable, it was also, from a medical perspective, quite unfortunate. Because hope was one thing but the child's condition had deteriorated far beyond the point of possible improve-ment. The end, to put it bluntly, was inevitable, and all that resistance could achieve now was a prolonging of pain. Their condolences, which had the echo of rote, weren't quite an apology, or an admission of failure, but accounted for part of the whole process, another box ticked, a duty done. And Michael and Barbara did what anyone would do, anyone who'd endured even a shard of what they were going through. They listened, took turns grasping at hands whenever hands were offered, and nodded their heads in all the right hollows to indicate understanding. Their stunned expressions encouraged the illusion of being somehow shielded, which suggested that they might yet make it through this without suffering too much in the way of collateral damage.

But once they were alone and their defences began to crumble, there was only pain. Against that, Michael used

43

silence as a guard and separated himself from the world with a wall of almost impenetrable thickness, but Barb wore her desperation openly, as nonsensical yearning. Planning for the future, for who and what their little boy would be, what kind of girl he might marry, how soon and how prodigiously he could be expected to make grandparents of them. And how complete he'd make their family, and their lives, once all of this was behind them. Michael hung his head but felt at a loss as to what he should do or say. So he said nothing. And then, one afternoon, he returned with pastrami and mustard sandwiches from a nearby street-corner deli, to find her on the ledge perched high above hysteria.

Tears fogged her vision so that when he spoke, when he asked her what was wrong, she had to find him with a flailing hand, her fingers bouncing off his chest and shoulder, patting her way up to his jaw. It took a full minute before she could answer and he had to bear through that minute, more afraid than he had ever been in his entire life. More afraid even than the time, in Buffalo, when he was mugged at knifepoint by two men, one of them white, the other Latino, men with the mark of heroin oozing from every pore. Craven types, jittery and wired, who flashed a wooden-handled steak knife with five or six nastily protruding inches of serrated blade even after he had given up his wallet. That was a sore loss too, not just the entire month's rent in cash which probably equated to a dozen fixes apiece for them if they shopped in the right place, but also the photo of Barb taken on the night of their first date, a beautiful fresh-faced Barb, young and smiling, nineteen years old and glowing with all the life yet to be lived. The Latino had nail holes for eyes and a crude Indian-ink tattoo spouting from the collar of his shirt and all the way up his neck and one cheek, the flames of an inferno morphing into a multi-headed serpent demon, and he was the one who brought the tip of the knife to the soft meat beneath Michael's chin, pressing until it hurt and then let a little blood, a small amount but enough to make it assault, or even some category that passed for more serious. And he just stared, teeth clenched, while the other one, shaven bald and with a face milk-white except for a cloudy spume of several days' beard growth, bounced back and forth from foot to foot, screaming with glee to do it, to go on and just cut the motherfucker's tongue out through his throat. Start with his tongue. At that moment, Michael had felt death upon him, death as an actual physical weight, and all he could do was close his eyes and try to nullify conscious thought, even as his mouth repeated over and over for them to take the wallet, repeating it even after the wallet was gone, wincing only when the knife's tip pierced him and drew blood, and wincing again when his attackers broached the idea of rape, of getting him into the alley and down in the dirt and the piss, him in that nice suit too, the fuck, and opening a train line on him. And somewhere between there and the few seconds later, after they had fled the scene, he had a picture in his mind, an absolute under-standing of how it was going to be, of how they would wrestle him into the alley and work him over, taking turns on him not because they wanted to particularly but because they could, and then, after they were done, how they would take the knife and pummel his chest and stomach, or rip up his throat, one of them holding his head back by a fistful of hair while the other took the blade on a sauntering loop clean and slow from one ear to the other. Even after they had run off at a stumbling gallop, whooping laughter back into the night, the sense of death had remained with him. Sometimes he doubted that the feeling of it ever really went away. Until James Matthew's condition worsened, this had been entire streets clear in any attempt at polling the worst moment of his life. But as bad from start to finish as the experience had been, the very fact that he had not died counted in the end for everything, that by providence or good nerve he had walked out of it, shaken, yes, and down some decent cash, but with his pulse, and his ass, still intact. Yet the terror he felt on that hospital afternoon, watching Barbara struggle to focus her eyes, to breathe, to speak and explain herself, was a thing worse by far and then by as far or further again.

She'd been thinking, she said, when her words finally found some definable shape. Beating herself up, actually. About the part she'd played in all of this, what she might have done to cause what was happening, or what she might have done differently. She'd taken a drink, more than one, in fact. More than a few. Back before she'd even been sure she was pregnant, yes, but ignorance was no excuse. And even when she did know, there'd still been the odd glass of wine in the night-time, with dinner or in front of Carson. What if it was the wine, or that morning when she felt a twinge while out shopping but shrugged it off as mere over-exertion or simply something she'd eaten? Or what if it was something else she'd done, they'd done? Sex, say, some position that changed all the rules?

Michael tried to understand but the talk as it came made no sense. Tears began again to clot her voice, to make a mess of her, but she kept on and he kept trying to listen, wondering all the while if he was missing some critical detail that would help clarify everything. He realised only gradually that she was rambling, that she'd become swamped in a fantasia of emotional self-flagellation. Desperate to apportion blame, she found herself to be the softest target.

'These things happen,' he told her, drawing her into his arms. Not meaning it, not really believing it, but wanting to try, nonetheless. Beyond the glass lay the tiny unconscious shape of their child, and their grip on him was coming loose. Some day soon, the whole of space would lie between them. The fear that had built and was choking Michael all at once fell away and left behind only a deep, perishing sense of despair. 'It's not your fault, Barb,' he said. 'It's nobody's fault. A glass of wine is not responsible for this. It's devastating, I know, but we have to lift ourselves up from this. We need to be strong.'

His voice had lost a lot of its belly and settled for scraping. Barb pressed her face to his chest and wept, and then after a while the tears abated and she looked up at him, nodded that she was all right now, that it was merely an aberration, a temporary eruption. He watched her, seeking signs, and to fend him off she smiled and raised herself for a kiss. He remembered for a long time afterwards exactly how, in that moment, her mouth felt against his. Pressing, eager for the connection. He could feel his own lips pushing back against his teeth in a way that was not comfortable but not painful either, just intense. That press and then, as she breathed, the invasion of her heat. Even after she'd pulled away, the sensation lingered. She smiled and he smiled back, and having without intent achieved sad matching expressions, they sat down on the two side-by-side pink plastic chairs and slowly worked their way through the sandwiches.

She needed to vent. Michael understood this, and even though it was frightening in the moment, he learned to bear it, knowing it would quickly pass and that she'd sooner rather than later steady herself again. There was probably even something terrifically healthy about it all, even if her fantasies did occasionally threaten to get out of hand. Like the night she had awoken from a sitting-up doze and cried for the greater part of an hour over the one-in-whatever possibility that their little boy might turn out to be gay. As if that was her mind's most pressing concern. The tears were not because of his potential homosexuality, she explained, when she could, but because of guilt at her own expectations and, okay, her selfishness. Shouldn't it be enough to have him in their lives, healthy and happy? Why would it matter if he was gay? It was a parent's duty to lend support, to nurture and care for and to reassure. The rest of the world would be judgemental enough without her adding to his pain. So why then was she already wishing grandchildren on him, why was she labelling him, boxing him into a life that he might not in all honesty want, or be able, to live? Her mind in such moments viewed the world as violently askew, and sent her wandering in mirror-walled labyrinths and fun-house mazes, where everything had more than one face and nothing was quite as it seemed. All that Michael could do when she got like this was hold back and just try to ride it out.

But everyone deals with crises in different ways. The small explosions allowed Barbara at least some degree of control over her situation, even if she could not directly affect the outcome. And most of the time she was the strong one. Her weak moments were anomalies in an otherwise stable outlook, which was why she probably nurtured them so readily and with such vigour. Michael, on the other hand, followed a different tack. He coped through a technique of repression. He could still function on an acceptable physical level but, as the hospital time built, he took to viewing everything from a step removed. Inside, he was carnage, but he was not the sort to cry. And after a while his face set itself to a new, blank expression. He could feel the muscles reshaping themselves, pulling downwards over the bones of his face, settling around the persistent clench of his jawline. Lack of sleep had a lot to do with it, but not everything. The rest, at least as much, was due to the strain of watching, especially after hope had begun to fade. It was a survival mechanism, a lockdown, the body anticipating some hard blow and bracing itself for the impact. Neither his technique nor Barb's passed muster as psychologically ideal, but then instinct follows no textbook.

Their world became the corridor, and they spent long hours at the glass, leaning in an effort to catch the movements of their little boy, the barely significant rise of the chest with each tiny intake of breath, each sip of sterile, purified air, and the inevitable exhalation's imagined whisper. Watching for breaths, certain that each would be the last, at least until the void stirred again.

Michael allowed himself little ground for optimism, and he wondered, in off-moments, if James Matthew would hate him for giving up so easily, or if God would, if his passive conspiracy would be taken as an act of treason against God's supposedly strictest rule, that of the sanctity of life? By simply standing here, was he effectively surrendering his soul in resignation? Because he knew how to talk. He was a salesman, for Christ's sake, he had the tools, the weapons. Talking was his business. He hadn't agreed with what was being done, yet held back from voicing an objection, from insisting that they do *something*, the doctors, the nurses, that they keep on trying, fuck the theories and scenarios and the projected outcomes, that they continue running the life support, keep on with the drip feed, the attempts at stimulating the lungs, the liver, the kidneys to some manner of workable life. But instead of speaking up, he accepted spectator status, and watched in the same way that spectators have always watched innocents march to a burning or to the gallows or the gas chambers. Or to the lions.

Where exactly did the line land between mercy and murder? Such a strain of thinking was nothing less nor more than the cracks of a mind in mid- to full-blown breakdown, but when the facts were magnified and distilled to the nth degree, the question screamed with abject insistence. Even as the seconds clocked up and beat by, he understood on a multitude of levels that this was one of his life's defining moments, one that would still churn for him when his own end wound finally into view.

The problem, one of the problems, was that the adrenaline had flushed from his system, leaving him with nothing to do but stretch out in the emptiness. While Barb elected to weep and scratch her way through, he dealt with the pain and doubt by boxing it up and burying it all to an unmerciful depth. The question of God, or of God's hand, in what was going on had to do with belief, and the answer, whether coming down on one side or the other, surprisingly evaded intellectuality, and simply was. In euphemistic terms, faith stood akin to allergy: you either suffered from it or you didn't. Some, finding themselves in this situation, raged hard against the notion of belief and dismissed such thoughts as worthless, replacing them with a determination to find their own way onwards, for better or worse. Others, by contrast, turned stupidly devout, Indian-burned with terror at the possibility that there might yet be more of this to come, floods more, and that in the grand scheme of things they could never be anything better than cowering specks, there wholly for the entertainment of an Almighty who ran the whole show by whim. And finally, for those few too dulled to face either extreme, there was a third option, the one where you accepted the limits of existing strictly within the current surround, and if you happened to think at all about the big questions, particularly the question of God as myth or reality, then you showed due care not to wade any further than a knee's worth of depth into that mire. This third choice was the path Michael felt offered the best chance of survival.

*

That last day, after some member of staff had adjudged that business was, for now, concluded, Michael and Barbara walked in silence from the hospital. Somehow, they had lost several hours. Morning seeped into afternoon, and the dusk of evening threatened. Details had gotten in the way: the busy work of papers to be signed, forms that had to be collected, filled in, delivered to particular departments, copied, collated, rubber stamped. Certificate of death, autopsy permissions and appointments for grief counselling that, despite their best intentions, they'd give up on after the second or third try, once the space for delusion had sufficiently diminished and it became clear that there was no ready-made cure, no matter what anyone said or did, not for something like this.

Michael led the way, trying hard to hold himself together, and Barb gripped his arm as they navigated the dim twists of corridor in search of an exit. In her free hand, in a small clear plastic bag that whispered with every pace against the stony denim of her thigh, she carried James Matthew's bagged effects. A neatly folded blue cotton jumpsuit and a lemon-coloured cardigan, neither of which had ever been worn; birth and death certificates; a single Polaroid snap, the image thick with clarity-denying reflection from the impeding layers of glass, but better than nothing; and a green plastic wristband with a name scrawled in inky blue block capitals. These few morsels of identification were the only physical evidence that their son had ever existed, but the bag's simple concision made it all somehow worse.

Outside, the fading day pressed a raw wet easterly wind into their faces, and somewhere between the hospital's doorway and where they had parked the car she let go and began to weep. A cloying carbolic stench clung to their clothes, hair and skin, enduring even through the wind. Washing would remove that smell, but not one wash, and not the impact of its memory. When Michael opened the car's passenger door for her she nodded and got in but the tears kept coming. After a minute or two of trying and failing to think of something good to say, some few pathetic words of comfort, he abandoned the cause, sat in behind the wheel and switched on the radio. In the years to come, that will seem like a particularly callous action, but the truth, at that moment, was something far more helpless, and maybe more pathetic. Because her crying was unbearable, the jagged shudders of breath, the whine that came stabbing up out of her in gouts from some deep place. Her soul in haemorrhage.

She sat with her head hanging and her hands cupped beneath her face to catch the tears, but he resisted the urge to look at her and instead reached out for the radio's dial and turned it slowly through patches of static and the occasional stuttering flare of noise until eventually a station came in clear and music flooded the car, hard and for a heartbeat or two shapeless without the rumble of the engine to temper at least the edges of its roar. The force of it caused his breath to catch in his throat and all he could do was sit back and watch the first scuds of rain mark and then mutilate the windshield while melody broke over him like tide across the spikes of a low reef. Van Morrison, first, 'You Make Me Feel So Free', fresh as the nightly news but already sounding stone-cold and classic, the rich gurgling bass and joyous sax stretching out in bedrock support beneath the expressive honey-soup resonance of vocals building towards ecstasy and then drawing back, sated, on soft, heaving promises.

It passed, leaving a moment of nothing: empty air and only the sound of his and Barb's strained breathing and the needle-tap of the rain on the glass, and then again the silence became snarled in the rise of another song, something older this time, something ancient-sounding. 'Gates of Eden', a sunken landmass once more breaching the surface, and Bob Dylan in full-throated strum. It was a song he knew well, or thought he did, from the years of nights spent spinning his scratched thrift-store copy of *Bringing It All Back Home* when he wasn't listening to Willie Nelson or something with more swamp involved, but he'd never before heard it so uncovered, the acoustic guitar hooked to an almost voodoo frenzy, the occasional harmonica scream and, most of all, the voice, everything, enormous, cleaved from rock, chipped and cracked but with the strength of standing stones and beautiful in the way that hard-wrought things can sometimes be, and as full of gospel truth as the very dirt itself, pushing prophesies or reportage of the most surreal revelation. Words of pure nightmare, too, peeling back the skin in full disclosure and leaving the listener among the end notes just a shy lean from madness.

He felt drained, blood-let. They both did. Barb found a full box of tissues in the glove compartment but struggled to stem the wash of tears. She sat there, head still bowed, clutching rags of the soft paper in one fist, but the continuing music cloaked what sounds she might have made and seemed instead to speak for her. And not knowing how else to respond, Michael closed his eyes and listened, as the words of the song came above the hammering guitar, a touch too loud but loud enough to obliterate thought, packing the air the way fog can. The interruptions of harmonica made sense now, crow-screams for everything lost, dense as stone with feeling and fissured with nearly unbearable despair.

When the song ended he could hardly move. He was trembling inside, vibrating. But his surfaces were numb. He switched off the radio and after a moment started the engine. It turned over once and stalled, then caught on the second try. They left the hospital grounds and drove back through the early-evening traffic, in the direction of home. The silence was worse than words, and it built and fermented between them as the whiteness was drawn like poison from the wounded day. Barb, in between waves of tears, sat half an arm's length apart, a small frail ruin, her wide eyes gleaming in the yellow glare of the street and tunnel lights. And understanding that talk couldn't help, he kept his attention fixed on the road ahead, braced in anticipation of some inevitable impact, certain that there was more to come, that there had to be. Not moving even to breathe, trying to be strong and not making it.

III

In the White Room

The room is small but immediately becomes theirs. Caitlin enters first, and glances round, feeding on detail. The nape of her neck is shown, just for a moment, as a white slope before she turns her head again and the loose curtain of her casual ponytail falls back into place.

Michael leans the weight of his body to the door until the lock clicks shut. He delights in watching her, a habit shaped by time, armour against the day she finally slips or is torn from his life.

She moves into space towards the bed, absorbing everything of this surround. Her expression rouses a sense of faded youthfulness, her eyes wide and almost scared, her mouth clenched but not her jaw, her body a straight, slender vessel full of so much past. She skirts the bed, drifts to the far side of the room, her coat, forgotten, inconsequential, dragging behind her in whispers across the cheap nylon carpet. When she moves into the frame of the window, the pale, smoky noontime light transfigures her. The effect is startling. Her skin turns the glassy frail of a porcelain screed, slightly translucent, hinting at the branches of bone beneath, and the memory of a dream stirs in Michael's mind, years old and long forgotten but suddenly real and clear again and soaked in precisely this same light, one that captured her beside a window much like this one, naked to the waist but with her hair still with all its young length and fullness cascading in dark flumes down over her shoulders and small breasts. Standing in profile, head down, she was counting coins, brown pennies, from one hand to the other. And she was weeping.

'Not too bad, is it?' She doesn't turn to look at him yet, and he knows why.

'No,' he says, lying out of duty. 'Not too bad at all. We've known worse.'

The room is clean and plain but determinedly sterile, with all trace of romance having been surgically removed, the sort of room suited to women on the run, and travelling salesmen, and those who wish to hide a while without being found, those who need time alone to think of good or even bad reasons why they shouldn't hang themselves in the closet or pull a razor blade across their wrists. But the cold strain of afternoon had added something more. It flushes through the tall, narrow sash window, a blanched, bulky light that thickens the air, melts surfaces and slows the very turning of the world. And against that, every past and possible future collide with a clap and fuse together.

They are held apart by more than distance. Her eyes find him as they find the corners, and the smile too is rubbed and faraway. 'Well,' she says, 'I like it. I don't know what it is, but the place speaks to me. I could write here. That's a thought I've not had in a long time. But this air is heavy with stories.'

Her stillness softens reality. To Michael's eyes, in the moment, she could pass for twenty-five again, young, pretty, still slim as gathered sticks, the woman of his dreams, for better or worse, smiling but with the sadness that never quite departs her and which always turns him ten kinds of soft. The room, he decides, will be sufficient for their needs, but only because they have carried love in here with them, in them. That, and perhaps the peculiar quality of the gifted light.

He settles on the bed's nearest corner. The mattress beneath him, understandable given the sort of traffic it must experience, has the firmness of blanketed steel. Standards here set their mark at perfunctory, the full scope of their ambition. Signs of tiredness and age catch and hold as small boasts to survival, like the licks of fur that can be found dappling the briary ditches of home on wet October mornings. Paint on the walls a watery buttermilk; a gauze of curtain boiled down to the grim shade and texture of dust; starched, papery bed sheets and a woollen throw, heavy as plywood, the pinkish tan of a pig's hide. At the foot of the bed, breaking the wall's barren monotony, a medium-sized mirror, oval and unframed, hangs full of his slightly magnified reflection, his thick bowed shoulders, his sallow face rutted with terminal dread. Bubbles rash the surface of the glass, the oxidised metal like brackish acne seeping through the silvering, but these flaws only enhance the accuracy of his depiction.

Instead of resisting the sight of himself, he sits and cultivates a state of calm, tries hard to make the pieces of who he really is fit inside the pieces of what he is finding in the glass. But he is too aware of the time. They have an afternoon, and the hours and minutes are finite. Still with his coat on, and in an awkward fashion that has become quite typical of him, he begins to undo the laces of his shoes. Recent years have seen him fall a long way out of shape, and the hunched posture reveals too much of his dishevelled self. A bluster of heat builds behind his face, reddening his skin, and his breathing turns strained and then splits open.

He slips off his shoes and sets them precisely together at the foot of the bed. When he looks up, Caitlin is studying him, his shoulders rounded and gone to fat, the pinkness of his scalp blushing through the tightly cropped salt-and-pepper hair, the first marked suggestion of a bald spot. That a shift in life stages has taken place can come as no sudden revelation; he has cleared the borders of middle age, and only the dead and the obscenely fortunate get to stay boyish for ever. But perhaps it is this light, white and cold, the soft strange ocean or grave-yard fog of Irish ghost stories, that offers some fresh perspective, or even some hint of her own first subtle crumbling, because there is a visible stiffening inside her smile. She averts her gaze but only gets as far as the mirror, and in not wanting to see any more she succeeds in seeing it all.

'I'm sorry it's not the Ritz,' he says, to the side of her face. He knows that her reflection is watching him, that they've made a triangle of the moment, but the angles don't spare them. 'You deserve the Ritz. You deserve better than I can give.'

'I don't need the Ritz,' she tells him, and all at once the hardness is gone, and the smile is hers again, the shape made for her mouth and eyes. 'I've never been that kind of girl. You must have me confused with someone else.'

'On the plus side, at least there are no cockroaches.'

'No roaches,' she agrees, glancing at the floor, just in case. 'Probably too cold for them.'

He laughs, because this is right, and then she laughs, too. When she moves to him, he leans back so that she can perch on his knee. She puts her arms around his neck, lacing her fingers together behind his head, and drawing close considers every aspect of his face. Then, like the punchline of a promise, she brings her mouth to his. This kiss differs from those that have gone before. The privacy of the room has set them free. She shifts for better purchase and he feels her body relax on one level and lift itself on another. He takes her lower lip very gently between his teeth and explores the feel of it with his tongue.

'Well,' she asks. 'Are you going to say it, or not?'

'Say what?'

'How you feel about me. How precious I am to you. That you've never loved anyone else the way you love me, and that you never will. That you'd stand in front of a lion for me. That if I needed a new heart you'd gladly give me the better half of yours.'

'My heart? You'd have to give it back to me first.'

She kisses him again, and with growing hunger leans into him and twists the fingers of one hand through his hair, running them against the grain. A trembling stirs in her. He can feel the beat of it through her body. Its reawakening gladdens him. His hand strays from her hip and traces a slow line up her side. She turns, slightly but with intent, manipulating herself against his touch so that it settles where she wants it to be.

'I love you,' he tells her, breathing the promise into her skin. He often delays giving her these words, toying with her in that way she likes, as if today will be the day that lust or passion causes him to forget. But he never has forgotten, not in all their years together. And he does not forget now.

She leans away, her breath carrying new weight. The skin at one corner of her mouth has begun to blush, angered to redness. He is the man she has known for so long, but there are times when the evidence of this seems slight, and she has to strain in order to assure herself that he remains unchanged. She cradles his chin and left cheek and with the pad of her thumb wipes away a gleam of saliva from his upper lip. On impulse, he opens his mouth and draws her in.

'Do you?' Her voice is hushed to the brusque above a whisper. 'Or do you only think you do?'

He opens the soft clench of his lips. Her escaping thumbnail taps his upper front teeth. He knows it makes no sound, yet he feels one. It lays a vibration into his tongue and the roof of his mouth.

'When it comes to love,' he tells her, trying to smile, trying to make less of the sensation, 'is there a difference?'

Her hand in his feels like the hand of a child. He examines it, scanning from the back of her wrist to the neatly trimmed moon-white crescents of her fingernails. The skin is pale and dry, thin as tissue paper but with none of that softness, soft only to the eye. Slats of bone press and grid the surface, and where the knuckles protrude the flesh pinches and darkens to some shade more defined. He traces these bones with his own fingertips. There is something of the galaxies about her substructure, cathedrals of mystery stretching beyond his comprehension, and every cell fascinates.

In contrast to all this detail, her palm has the skin of a gourd. The lines that do exist seem faint, as if time has eroded them the way wind smooths and polishes rock, though he is aware that this may be due to a failing of his eyesight rather than an actual fact. At work, glasses have become a permanence, as much a part of the uniform as the collar and tie or the patent leather shoes. Without them, the edges run, and while he resists wearing them in front of Caitlin, red pinches straddle the bridge of his nose. She is not a fool but, for either his sake or her own, lets it go unmentioned. There are, he supposes, enough surface objections already, without the need to acknowledge any more.

He opens her hand towards the window's light, which helps. The lines clarify themselves somewhat, though continue to hold their immediate codes intact.

Years ago, and prompted by some passing fancy, he'd read a book on palmistry. The bulk of what he learned has been long since lost, but he does recall a sense of the significance attributed to the three major lines. He knows, too, that this, her right hand, is her dominant hand. The lines of her left are, at least according to the lore, marks that she carried with her into the world and which speak of her potential as a person, of the talents and faults she was gifted and cursed from birth to possess. But her right hand tells of who she is now, who she has become through a melding of choice and fate, and these are the lines that also suggest who she might yet be.

Trawling his memory, he reads what he can, starting where everyone always starts, with the lifeline, which arcs in a generous loop around the pad of palm at the base of her thumb. This is a game, but he treats it as more than that.

'Interesting.'

She smiles. He sees it through her fingers, the edges of her teeth and the smallest pink tease of tongue.

'What is?'

'Oh, nothing. Just opening up a few of your secrets.'

'And?'

'Don't worry. I'll give you a chance to confess.'

To those who believe, everything means something: the length and sweep of the lines, their depth and intersections. Her heart line, which dictates not only health but love, runs in high, confident manner from the outer edge of her hand before curling to an end just beneath the index finger's root. There is evidence of a forking too, part of the way across, with a defined second prong that follows the mainline along in lower accompaniment and then at a roughly midway point quite abruptly stops.

A crater of dread opens up inside him. To bury it, or to hold it in, he brings his mouth to her skin. His lips track her fate lines, trying to follow their lead, hoping for some kind of understanding. And it occurs to him that after all these years he has stumbled upon an entirely new part of her to kiss.

She responds to his mouth with small hiccups of laughter. But her eyes have tightened with anxiety.

'Since when can you read palms?'

'I'm part Gypsy. Did I forget to tell you?' He grins, then begins to nuzzle her wrist. He can only imagine her pulse against the tip of his tongue, though it feels no less real for that.

Her free hand beats at his shoulder. 'Asshole.'

His grin widens, but his efforts don't falter. He kisses his way gently along the inside of her forearm and she watches, feeling the damp and softness of his mouth and, beneath it, the scrub of his chin, its shave already hours outgrown. And even as she again coaxes the fingers of her free hand through his hair and, smiling with pleasure at the very completeness of his efforts, pinches the waxy lobe of his right ear with little playful tugs, she is thinking of the Chakra points, remembered from a one-time yoga flirtation, and in particular of the palm Chakra. Illustrated in every derivative text as a large peering hieroglyphic eye fringed in beautiful comb-tooth lashes, it is said to act as the channel for administering and receiving medicinal energy. Michael's attention to his task, with such determination trying to kiss away all her worries and fears, all of her life's negative residue, at once amuses and impresses her, and while the act is not in itself particularly stimulating, not the way his mouth and teeth against the nape of her straining neck or nuzzling at the small of her back, or better still, between her legs, can be, the gesture in itself feels precious. Her smile hangs on, even as something shifts and turns suddenly warm inside. She pulls her hand back and they come together again, their bodies folding into one another's arms. She shifts her weight and begins to kiss his cheeks and eyes and the flesh rumpled in such hard concentration just above his nose.

'So,' she says, sighing the words. 'You love me. Well, if it's any consolation, I'm afraid the feeling's mutual.' But even as she speaks, she is drawing herself back and rising from his lap.

Michael gazes up at her; his face is boyish in the moment, wide open and devout, bleached with insecurity.

'Then I suppose we're stuck with one another.'

She shrugs and reawakens her smile, or widens what is already there, a smile as vague as smoke, and when tears start to threaten she stoops and kisses him again but turns away before he has time to open his mouth and drifts once more around the corner of the bed to the window.

Immediately on peeling back the net curtains, the afternoon thins. Touching the nets leaves a film of dust, real or imagined, on her fingertips, and she rubs them clean in an absent fashion against her thigh, then leans straight-armed on the shallow sill and brings her face to within inches of the glass.

Back when Coney Island still counted worth a damn, the hotels out here were all silk and roses, existing as genuflections towards true luxury. The men wore fine suits to come here, and the women, even the molls, floated. Swing and big-band music decked the days and nights, small talk passed in fifties and hundreds, folding money, and you named your poison in whispers and with a certain kind of knowing look. But that was then, once upon a time. The passing years and decades cleared those decks, along with bangs and pocket watches and sterling silver cigarillo holders, and what remains now is basic, perfunctory, clean in that ugly, ravaged way of old and over-washed things. Good enough still for an hour or two but not for much longer. Deals are done in cash, because credit cards only complicate matters and tend to embarrass the takers and givers alike. Money buys you four walls and a bed, but what it really buys you is the bed, and a piece of afternoon for putting it to best possible use.

This third-floor vantage peers out across a scrub of wasteland towards the ropy spindles of a lopsided and long-abandoned roller coaster. The view is apparently complimentary. Having slowed towards a standstill at this time of year, the hotel's proprietors are, it would seem, grateful for any custom, no matter how sordid or fleeting. Gazes here are trained to looseness. Nothing lingers, aware of what could be exposed, and they don't believe in questions, because the risk is high that they will not like the answers. Today, the view probably feels like the least they can do. Left of the ruined joyride and some hundred yards or quarter of a mile further on, the upper half of a Ferris wheel's candy-coloured exoskeleton perches, like some fossilised remains from prehistory, against the rise of the land. And unseen, but present in every pore of afternoon, the endless cant of ocean slopping in against and back from the shore. Caitlin's breath presses the glass, mist forms and evaporates, adding further texture to the day. When she notices, she etches out the crude depiction of a smiley face, a quick imperfect circle, two jabbed dots for eyes and a long, debonair curl of mouth. The image survives a few seconds, then recedes to nothing.

'Can you believe how long we've been coming out here?

'More years than it's probably right to count.'

'I know every stick and stone of the place, at this point. I could walk these streets blind without a single wrong step. And yet, there's something about it that makes every time feel like my first time. Why do you suppose that is?'

'Because you keep seeing it from different angles. The fresh balances out the familiar.'

She turns from the window and leans back against it. Michael, still sitting on his corner of the bed, is undressing in an absent fashion. He has shed both his overcoat and sports coat, and the belt of his trousers hangs unbuckled. A few of his shirt buttons have been picked open, exposing a wedge of white thermal undershirt with a rounded neck-line, but whether through apathy or distraction his fingers have lost interest in their task. His hands are settled now in a loose splay, one on each knee, and his gaze has become stuck in the middle distance.

'Well,' she says, 'I keep seeing you from different angles, too. But you don't change at all, except that the view has gotten so old.'

The weight of the following silence tips him out of his trance. He comes back in stages, looks at her and finally shrugs, not seeing the joke. Set against the window as she is, the light has reduced her, softening layers, bringing her down to a core. All he can think about is how beautiful she looks; how, on her, the years have meant nothing. It

68

thrills and saddens him. They have the afternoon, and they've enjoyed a lot of these days, but he also knows that they should have made so much more of their time together, and they should have fought harder against the time spent apart. The problem, obvious in hindsight, was that they'd been too willing to ration their longings and too readily accepting of their lot, and only now, at this settled age, can they recognise that the turning of the world has spun them loose of some essential mooring. These few snatched hours, once the preserve of love or of something inseparably close to love, have become a pretence at satisfaction.

'Christ,' she says, 'it's like the Yukon in here. You'd think they could afford to burn a nickel's worth of heat on the place. How do they even expect to stay in business, inflicting this kind of cold on their guests?'

She rubs her arms in a brisk gesture from shoulder to elbow, then cups her hands together and sighs into them. The room is not really that cold, but the air in here does have a rawness to it, and if her action is exaggerated then it also makes a valid point. The problem, of course, is that the cold has followed them in from the street.

'Coffee, I think. To fire the fire.'

There is a plastic jug-shaped electric kettle on the dressing table, grape green in colour, perched on a round tray that also holds a pair of cups upturned on almost matching saucers, a scattering of sugar and coffee sachets and a few capsules of chemical creamer. The display could be part of a stage set, a modernist commentary on the instant and the artificial. Art for art's sake, a stillness devoid of life.

Michael is again attending to the buttons of his shirt. She watches his thick fingertips pick their way down over his stomach and thinks that the sitting posture does him no favours.

'It'll take more than coffee to fire my fire,' he says. 'With this cold we'll be doing well to raise a puff of smoke.'

Concentrating on his chore, he misses the offer of her smile. And beyond the window, the sky is turgid with the lumpen alabaster finish of a coming storm.

'Let's give the coffee a shot first,' she says. 'Then we can see how we stand.'

She fills the kettle with water of questionable freshness from a tall, uncorked glass bottle that is already only three-quarters full, but when she taps the switch high up on the handle, a red light sparks and immediately dies. She shifts the switch again but nothing happens.

'Shit.'

'What?'

'The kettle. It won't come on.'

'Try it again.'

'I did.'

'Keep trying.'

'I did. I am.' Her thumb rocks the switch open and closed. 'It won't come on.'

Michael peels off his shirt and folds it with care, tucking the collar beneath his chin and extending the arms. Neatness matters to him. Caitlin thinks he is too obsessive in this. Barbara also thinks so, though she has long since stopped mentioning it. But he can't help himself. It's not a question of vanity but of order. The alternative – chaos – would be, for him, unbearable.

'Wait,' Caitlin says, raising one hand.

'What now?'

'I don't understand. The light is out, but it seems to be working.'

She leans in a little closer. Her hand continues to hang raised to one side of her, pressing the air. Michael stops what he is doing and also strains to listen. Within seconds, a small but distinctive whispering announces itself, rustling beneath the stillness, and then the first thread of steam begins to seep from the kettle's spout. The light is an indicator, there to grant reassurance to the eye, and plays no part in the kettle's ability to function, yet for reasons she cannot understand, its absence has stirred awake a peculiar unease.

'A bulb must have gone,' Michael says, as much to himself as to her, but his words are merely the ready acceptance of learned facts. And even the world was flat until someone decided otherwise.

She nods, but remains troubled by the thought that ignorance is not blissful at all, but reckless.

He takes off his watch, brings it out of habit to his ear, then proceeds to wind it. Few watches need winding any more, but his has some age and fits a different category. And because it belonged to his father, its value can only properly be measured in terms of sentiment.

Once, some years back, he'd spoken a little bit about it as they lay in bed. She'd asked. They'd reached the cusp of some landmark life barrier, a notable anniversary of their initial coming together or maybe a thirty-fifth or fortieth birthday, one of those events that seems to count for so much until the next one arrives and renders it obsolete, and at that time, as well as they'd come to know one another, there was still much that remained unfathomed. They lay in one another's arms, weary and content, with the sweat of their exertions cooling on their skin, chatting in that soft manner of dreams about things they owned, material possessions that they'd save first from fire should the need ever arise.

'The watch,' he'd admitted, after a moment's thought. 'I know it's not much to look at, but it counts for something.'

She'd reached across his chest and lifted it from the bedside locker. A steel-bodied thing, cheaply made and cold to the touch, with a frayed hide strap and a glass front so badly chipped and abraded that reading the time always involved a high element of guesswork. He let her scour it for secrets, then eased it from her hands and considered it himself.

'Whenever I look at this,' he said, 'I feel like I'm a child again. I can see the old kitchen as clear as rainwater in my mind: the transistor radio keeping out the silence and my father at the breakfast table, turned towards the window for the early light or hunched close to the lantern, his eyes straining and his awkward fingertips trying to synchronise the time with the first news of the day. Even back then the watch haemorrhaged seconds, but it ran, I suppose, as best it could, and it got to know a bit of life and too much in the way of death. The old man would wind it, and then he'd press it to his ear and incline his head until he felt confident that the beat was holding steady. It was his routine, but it was also more

72

than that. It was how he grounded himself against whatever the day would bring, either in the fields or out on
the water. And sometimes he'd notice me looking and
bring it to my ear too, and I'd either close my eyes
and listen or else concentrate hard on his smile. "Like a
heartbeat," he'd say, and I always knew what he meant,
not even the words but the way he said it, proud and
with a certain amount of compassion, and then he'd
stand, push a hand into the small of his back and stretch
away the knots, before reaching for his coat.'

'That's a nice memory,' she'd said. 'You're lucky to
have it.'

But Michael shook his head.

'It's more vivid than just a memory. It's as if I've only
now lived it, or that I'm living it still. And maybe that's
the truth. Because the past is never really past for us, is
it? I think it's always there, inside us but always near the
surface. The watch is a key to a particular door, useful
for opening up that part of myself again. Other reminders
open other doors. There's something soothing about that
but, the truth is, it also turns me a little cold.'

Based on the things he'd said, and what she'd learned
about the place from books, she understood his Inishbofin
to be, at least back then, somewhere that turned its men
old in a hurry, that aged them hard against rain and gales.
And it was a place difficult to abandon in any way other
than the physical. Until about ten years ago, when the
sheer morbidity of the practice finally registered with him,
he'd kept a small creased photograph of home tucked
away in the back of his wallet. His father's name was Seán,
and the picture caught him on some bright day, coming

in from the fields or from the boat, decked out in a flat knitted wool cap and a heavy black overcoat worn open across what looked to be a strong chest. He bore a certain resemblance to Michael, mainly in the shy and almost forlorn twist of his mouth and the way in which he pinched his eyes against the sun. She knew how deeply Michael hurt with the thought of how the old man had had to die alone, in the westernmost corner of the low field behind their cottage, on a damp late February evening after a few hours spent turning the soil of his potato drills in preparation for the planting of some earlies. He'd probably straightened up from his work and lingered as he often did to gaze out over the undisturbed emptiness of the ocean, seeing the water placid that day, stretching silver and smoke-blue towards the unseen raft of America and the suggestion of a setting sun. No one even missed him until the Thursday night, when he failed to show up at Hickey's for his usual couple of pints and the few hands of forty-five, and he was not found until the Saturday morning, nearly five full days after his passing. His heart had given out and he'd fallen in a ditch, and when they finally found him, a few of the neighbours checking the bottom field as a last resort after they'd already swept the island and scoured the reefs around the nearby cliffs, they knew him for certain only by his clothes and the old sandalwood rosary bead that he held clutched in one hand, because rats and crows had already taken the buttery pulp of his eyes and much of the flesh from his nose, cheeks and throat.

Áine had written, but the letter took its time in finding Michael. By then, he'd already been gone nearly two years, and on most days Inishbofin still felt like the only reality. New York was not at all as he'd expected it to be, and until the letter arrived, home's final tether had yet to give. But now, with such news, there could be no going back, and nothing much to go back to. He was working, but not steadily, labouring three and sometimes four days a week for a small-time subcontractor, a Dublin man named Hallissey who paid below the going rate but who at least paid in cash, no questions asked, so he was surviving. The bedsit apartment, all he could then afford, was a dive, a real step down even the most unreliable of ladders. The water coughed and rattled in the pipes, great shrouds of mould had to be scraped from the bedroom's window wall every couple of weeks, and the apartment two doors down housed a young African male prostitute who was often to be found in the mornings either passed out in the hallway with his jeans down around his knees and a piece of hose rubber knotted tightly above one elbow, or else perched on the top step of the stairs, elbows on knees, rocking gently back and forth heaving with tears.

'My father would still have died,' Michael said, when Caitlin pressed. 'Even if I'd been there. The inquest described it as a massive coronary. But it wasn't instant. I know that field, every clod of earth. He'd have made for the ditch in order to rest until the worst of it eased. The pain would have caused him to pass out, but even so he probably took as long as an hour to go. If I'd been there he could at least have died with a bit of dignity. I could have held his hand the way he'd held my mother's, and he could have gone into the grave looking like himself. He shouldn't have been alone.'

'It's not your fault,' Caitlin told him, but he just shrugged.

'We always tell ourselves that, don't we? We try to absolve ourselves of guilt, or to at least lift ourselves above it. But that's wrong. Because we're never innocent. I had a responsibility to him. A duty.'

'You had a responsibility to yourself, too. And to those you love now. You still do. We all do.'

They could talk like this, in the way of people newly coupled, because the ground between them had not yet muddied. A shared bed narrowed the margins of their perspective, and brought everything into apparent proximity. And with every edge so clearly defined, relative youth made it possible to hold onto the pretence that a love like theirs was easy, something hardly more than a matter of decision. The sight of Michael, even just the sound of his voice on the telephone, was enough to light her up, but she understood even then that what she saw and heard was only part of the man in full, little more than the tarnished casing. So they advanced with care, hopeful and cautious as to what might lie ahead, and they chipped away at one another, particularly during the aftermath moments of lovemaking, when they felt at their most intimate. Bruising the skin, over and over, with questions, each seeking out better ways to plumb the other's depths.

Michael was at that time still grieving the loss of his little boy, still in so many ways braced against the shock of that, even as months became a year and then longer, and he gave himself up only in spurts, coming to the facts as half-remembered things. His life, his past,

76

the people who had decked his wake. He spoke in a casual way, insinuating into the words a certain lack of importance, maybe trying to temper the impact of their revelation, even then and out of some harsh lesson already learned trying to hold back some essential aspect of himself. But images, splinters of the past, broke the surface and took their own shape, demanding attention. There was the small lump that his father had on the back of one wrist, a ganglion cyst, and how, having read of the most efficient treatment, the old man stretched out his hand, palm down, on the kitchen table and insisted, against his daughter's pleas, that seven-year-old Michael slam the lump with a hulking leather-bound Bible. Because it needed to be a Bible. And, incredibly, it had worked; such faith was rewarded, but in that typically perverse way of most answered prayers, with the cyst being temporarily consumed in the great engorging swell caused by two shattered metacarpals. Or the unembarrassed baths that he and Áine had been made to take together as young children, and the glimpses he'd caught of the chocolate thumbprint birthmark on the high inside part of her thigh as they sat, knees bent and face to face, in the large green tin basin that had to be hauled in from the back yard and set before the blazing fire every second Sunday night of winter. The water was heated in pans on the range, and while their mother soaped their small thin bodies and their nests of tangled hair, they played like harpies, incessantly screaming about the cold and kicking and splashing one another in an effort to reclaim a few important inches of lost foot space. And there was the morning that he and Áine had found the decomposing carcass of a dolphin or porpoise washed up on one of the Westquarter's deserted shingle beaches. Days dead in the water had seen it pulped beyond easy identification, but the damage confined itself mainly to the creature's upper torso and the tail half had survived nearly intact. Decked in kelp, the dark lower skin gleamed with a suggestive iridescence in the smoky springtime light, and the ridged, grit-speckled tail flukes lay with the wide-open elegance of a Japanese fan or the unfurled wings of some creature from myth, and it had been no trouble at all to convince themselves and one another that what they'd stumbled across was actually the corpse of a mermaid. At Áine's suggestion they'd knelt and sung to her, high keening funereal wails delivered in an Irish that was largely just sound because neither one of them knew enough of the lamenting words to properly lead. And afterwards, after they had finished their song and carried out a thorough examination of their find, they hauled the remains some twenty paces up the beach and set to hollowing out a grave above the high tide line, he digging with his hands, Áine using a piece of driftwood, having decided that even creatures of the sea deserved the dignity of a Christian burial.

Caitlin listened, and learned to cultivate her own masking sense of calm, even as she hoarded the scatter-shot details, each morsel a feast in itself but suggestive, too, of so much more. Every trail of recollection revealed something else of who he was, and she measured and tallied the pictures in her mind with the few photographs she'd seen. When speaking of his father, there was always sorrow in Michael's voice, a crazing of guilt. Even after so long. But there was also clear evidence of love, and of unflinching admiration.

She wished, often aloud, that she could have had a chance to meet the old man, just to shake his hand, to kiss his cheek, to sit with him and talk about the small things that they unknowingly shared as well as the things that were unique in the purest ways imaginable to each alone. Long after his death, these second-hand memories of him continued to fascinate.

'I honestly don't know how he'd have taken us,' Michael said once, after she'd pushed him on the subject. 'Towards the end, the last year or maybe two, certainly before I left, he had turned back to the Church. Not that he'd ever strayed too far away, and I'd be stunned if he missed a single Sunday morning Mass his entire life, but even though the teachings were fairly deeply ingrained I don't think religion ever properly took with him until the very end. Even then, it was probably more of a support mechanism than anything else, because there's comfort to be had in actively keeping the faith. But there'd have been the question of Barbara. He was never the judgemental type and he'd been through enough to understand that right and wrong are not always laid in straight lines. I do know that he'd have adored you. If the old man had a type, you'd be it. But it's circumstances. You can see that, can't you?'

She could. And she could also see what Michael was not saying but still meaning, which was that even in situations of impossible hypothesis no son wants to be thought badly of in his father's eyes, no son ever wants to disappoint. What she and Michael have together could very well pass for love, but it is also, by its very definition, adultery. They might prefer to define it otherwise, but there can be no denying the fact of that dirty little word. And the odds were probably a coin toss as to whether or not an old fisherman would have understood, or would have even wanted to understand.

There is something both pathetic and endearing about the way Michael sits here now, on the bed's edge, chewing on the right corner of his lower lip. His upper body has, in recent years, thickened with fat. The undershirt is of the sleeveless style and bulges around his breasts and, only in part because of his sitting posture, is dragged tight across the great bloat of his stomach. The watch looks small between his fingertips, yet she knows his touch to be delicate and always considered. Then, just as the water in the kettle stirs towards boiling point, he stands, opens the buttons of his pants and lets them slip to the floor.

His expression is one of studied embarrassment. He knows she is watching him. She wants to look away, for his sake, but cannot. His body keeps no secrets; from statuesque to an entirely different kind of artful, she has accompanied the evolution, or devolution, and is as familiar with his flesh as she is with her own. Yet his blush is genuine. She stands there, watching and thinking of things that she can say, such as how much she loves him, and how it pleases her to savour the details of who he is. But she holds back, not because these thoughts aren't true but because they do not feel like enough of the truth. At least, they won't to him. Anything she says now will make him feel worse than he already does. So she keeps silent, and she looks because to do otherwise will have an effect similar to words.

Then his stare meets hers, and they connect. She sees him as his surfaces declare: wilting and slumped, thick-shouldered, hair beginning to thin, face wrenched by middle age. But there is a second shade in evidence too, one that perhaps only she can recognise. It is there, twisted into the details of his features, in the shadowy furrows beneath his eyes, in the shifting pinch of his narrow mouth, and it reveals him in full, a childlike innocent needing her as no one ever has, a man still strong to an inch beneath the skin but weak with insecurity that she will one day see him for what he has become, and reject him. It hurts to acknowledge what time and life have done to him, how he has begun to fade. The day is coming when he'll be lost to her, and even when they have fallen far apart and can inform one another's lives only as memory, she knows that his absence will cause a catch in the very turning of her world. She looks at him and it is as if a veil has fallen away because she can see it all, the various pasts and futures superimposed against his bodily self, layered like auras of state. What she wants to say is that, instead of being repulsed by his flaws, they hold for her a kind of elemental beauty. All of this is what makes him real for her in a way that no one else has ever so fully been, and she finds herself again over-whelmed by the furnace blast of love that even the merest hint of him can awaken. Her breath hacks her throat. Tears press her surface, threatening floods. He either fails to notice or elects not to.

'Coffee,' she whispers, needing to look away.

She rights the cups on their saucers, rips open a couple of coffee sachets and pours in the boiling water. Without asking, she adds a pod of creamer to his, and two of the little paper envelopes of sugar. She stirs, and the mixture turns the colour of sand.

When she looks again she finds him still sitting, though he has shed his socks now, and also his boxer shorts. The undershirt, still in place, covers most of what he has going but not everything. She lowers her eyes in a fun, brazen acknowledgement and smiles, because it feels like the thing to do but also because the situation, clear of societal dictates as to what classifies beauty, has turned quite suddenly and unexpectedly sweet. Beyond the window and walls a world hangs in wait, but for now it has ceased to matter. In here, together, nothing is hidden. He looks at her and she wonders if he knows, if he suspects. She is sure he does. Now is the time to speak, to say what needs saying and have it over with, have everything over. But she cannot. This moment is too perfect. He perches there before her, worse than naked. The undershirt makes a difference, concealing his shame, softening his insecurity at having fallen so far out of shape. Even using the rawness of the room as an excuse to keep it on is an exposure of sorts.

'It's cold to be sitting there like that,' she says. 'You don't want to catch a chill.'

He meets her eyes, then laughs. The sound he makes is sharp, a jolt that hits and then stops.

'Does it show?' he asks, and without waiting for the kickback of a response gets up and moves around the bed. Farcical in his nonchalance, his ass for a second or two exposed bare and heavy, he pulls back the sheets on the side nearest the door and crawls in.

They drink their coffee, out of duty. Caitlin sits on the edge of the bed and notes with disappointment but not surprise its lack of give. The mattress is necessarily firm, without the promises of comfort, sweet dreams, or magic. It is yet another nod towards pragmatism, further evidence of the cold efficiency that caters to their kind of custom. Around here, promises have such a bad habit of not coming true, and expectation has proven the downfall of far too many.

Michael sips and winces. He tries but his eyes cannot keep a secret, and he abandons the cause at a little over halfway through, sets his cup on the bedside locker, and leans back into his nest of pillows, lacing his hands together behind his head. Happy to be watched, she keeps on, raises the cup and, just beneath it, the saucer, and drinks the way a bird will, pecking sips. Concentrating on the heat. The foul coffee coats her mouth, every forced swallow dragging with it a sour aftertaste, nasty in the way that instant can often be when you've become used to better. Not so long ago, their bodily hungers would have abided no such trifling distraction as coffee, but the gales of time have done for a lot of edges.

She feels very small beside him, and not just in a physical way. Safe too, sheltered, and happy at being desired. He says nothing. His patience seems unwavering. And it is as if time has stopped for them. The light of the afternoon washes over the bed, its blunt whiteness soaking every surface – the sheets, the walls, their bodies – with a soapy, deadening hue. Propped up by the pillows, he looks comfortable, but he is not smiling. The flesh of his bare arms and shoulders looks hard and smooth, like the stained marble of certain old fireplace fronts. Smoked from purity yet oddly clean, and with that sort of immaculate permanence. She has a sudden and almost unbearable longing to reach out for him, not in a sexual way but simply to wallow in the touch of his body, that flesh, to use her mouth on him, to taste his flavour. Black thatches of hair tuft his armpits, frail darkish crop circles suggest themselves through the thin white cotton of his undershirt where his tiny nipples poke to make their presence known. It amuses her, and in equal measure serves to break her heart just a little bit, that even after the hundreds of intimate occasions they have shared he still remains so bashful and embarrassed to be all the way naked for her. In physical terms, the years, particularly the last five or six, have not been kind to him. He carries an excess of weight now, and his stomach, which had been flat as paper when they'd first started going together, now presses and gently pummels her with every embrace. The fact that she minds this far less than he does, that actually she rather enjoys the snug closeness of it, the impacting security, is of no consequence. She has tried, often, to tell him this, sometimes making light of it, more times approaching the subject from its serious side, but his insecurity has closed him off to such words. He can't accept her reassurances, so he elects to wear the shirt.

And she, for her part, has learned to let it go. Foolishness cannot always be explained; sometimes there is nothing else to do but accept. Age brings wisdom only to the fortunate, and his age is showing hard now, and has been marked by a notable downturn in his general health. Aside from the inevitable surface deterioration, the failing eyesight, the complications of excess weight, he's become prone to worrying bouts of bronchitis, which seem to cling for months at a time, and is on daily medication for an angina problem still blessedly in its formative stages but which nevertheless fills her with unease at what menace might lie ahead. The details go unmentioned, except when avoidance is not an option, when the problems penetrate their cocoon. He doesn't discuss this with her, though he has mentioned it on two occasions. Once, a year and a half ago, because he'd had to put their arrangement back by a week in order to make a hospital appointment; and then again, several months later, when the initial medication was not correcting his levels to the doctors' satisfaction and they'd admitted him for a couple of days and put him through a range of tests in order to accurately adjust the dosage. Both times, he spoke with Caitlin about the angina in the same way that he might speak of the weather, or some book he'd read or film he'd recently seen. She listened and nodded, shrugged when shrugging was required, understanding exactly how far she could push and how far he could be pushed before the cracks broke his surface.

She keeps at the coffee now until its dregs catch as grit between her teeth, then tight-jawed with triumph returns her cup and saucer to the dressing table and proceeds to peel away her clothes. Her own movements are devoid of shyness. Familiarity and an earned trust have set her free. She unbuttons her blouse, works open the clasp and short zip at the left hip of her skirt, her expression for the most part serious, attentive to her task, but softening to a hinted smile when she glances once towards the bed and finds Michael's gaze nailed in place.

Her body has weathered the ageing process well, and she is proud of the way she looks, but even back when everything had still been fresh and new and exciting, her nakedness never bothered her. Even at her best, pragmatism had seen her set her own bar, unconcerned with highlight or flaw and without any grounds for hyperbole or hysterics. Her beauty has always been genuine but tends towards the ambiguous, there but reliant on the moment and the right beholder, and on angles, a precise tempo of pulse or a particular aspect of light in certain wane. And even on the down days that see her beauty further reduced, when she is caught in a cold or when an occurrence at home has clouded her mind, Michael knows what to look for and where to find it. Because there is always some moment in even the worst afternoon when she'll half-lid her eyes in answer to something he says, or in hesitation against some promise will let her mouth slip open to reveal the pink tip of her tongue over the rim of her lower teeth. Sometimes in bed, and touched just right, she'll arch her back so that the lattice of her ribcage better defines itself above the fallen suck of her stomach, and her small breasts quiver with each gulped breath and somehow expand, or at least seem to take all focus, to own the focus, her exposed nipples rough and stony hard as unripe berries but pressing the air, insistent, flourishing, engorged. As a couple, they have learned to live for instants, those heartbeats when a cowl falls away and her light shines through, and the rest of the world ceases then

86

to exist and there is only them, together, not only connected but fused.

Compared with the languid Barbara, a woman so perfectly formed as to be hardly made of flesh at all but rather of gossamer and ivory, perhaps of glass, some substance hard and full of sheen and in its way eternal, her own modest, even slightly boyish figure has always fallen a clear rank short, a rank at the very least. And when the sun was hot and the summer clothes were out, the distance between them measured in yards, not inches. Yet in the naked state, or in close approach, stripped down to the satin rose underwear that she owns and sports exclusively for Michael and which always makes her feel so good, she finds herself overcome with a confidence that only rarely invades the rest of her life any more.

It has less to do with love itself than with the degrees of love. With Thomas, her husband, what she has is a soft kind of love, something that has been watered down by time until the nature of it feels no longer enough. Thomas is a good man – a better man, perhaps, than she deserves – but he drums to a practical beat, and love to him means saucepans for Christmas, or steak knives, love to him is another bullet point on a long list, and never a priority. For some women, this would be acceptable, because other things matter, too, and, for some, matter more. Things like security, the comfort earned by hard work, the nice place and possessions, the yearnings for comfort met or at least acknowledged. These are all things that can speak of love, but only a kind of love.

Michael is different. What they have going is not just about the physical. With him, she can be the version of herself that she hopes and likes to believe is the real her. His flaws are worth enduring for what he brings to her world, and for the way he makes her feel, for the way he lets her feel about herself. Feminists might scream that no woman needs a man in order to be so fulfilled, but they – the militant among them, at least – refuse to see that not every woman is the same, or strong all the time. For the likes of her, it is in the small but explosive bursts of passion that all of life's truly worthwhile living gets done. More than anything else, it is his absolute consideration, his awareness and recognition of her as a person, whole and complete, that counts for so much, counts maybe for everything. From the first moment he brought her into his arms, she has understood just how much he cherishes her, how much every crease and bump and hollow of what she has to offer is worth to him.

She reaches back and unhooks her bra, taking her time for his benefit, loving the fact that he is watching, and going slowly, turning her shoulders slightly as a tease, giving him every chance to prepare. They have paid for their piece of day with this in mind, though they've learned to keep their expectations tempered. Every step of a dance is still the dance. The thermostat is sluggish in doing its job, and the chill of the room stings.

This is the moment for music. They both grin at once, the train of their minds hitting a kind of tandem step. She shakes her hips in exaggerated provocation and he scat-sings a bar or two of something bawdy, all throat-grunts and gibberish syllable-sounds. Then he draws back the blankets on her side of the bed, and she hurries to him at a little skipping run and plunges into his embrace.

From here, the sex just happens. Something about her face propels him, a particular angling of her cheekbones and chin that catch the heavy light in a certain way. They kiss, eyes closed, hard enough to hurt. But stopping is not an option. She gasps, surrendering to his lead, as they momentarily break apart, a flat papery breath that turns audible even into its fading. His hands coat her body, her breasts first, gripping the flesh in a gentle but assured way, taunting the nipples with little strokes and plucks, then sliding down over her ribs to the jut of her hips. He talks, in whispers that bore into her, because it is one of the things he likes to do and because he can't help himself, needing the approval of voice. Not words, exactly, or not identifiably so, but still in some language that she seems to understand, because in reply, or response, she tips her head back and catches his heartbeat kicking against her, through her, not just in one place but all over. She closes her eyes, opens them again when she feels his thumbs poking under the elastic of her panties. She tries to help but he eases her hand away and takes control of stripping her down. Working her body naked becomes easy once she yields. A game in itself.

The play that follows then is not exactly one for the manuals, but the details are unimportant. Better by a stretch than what has often marked their trysts in recent years, and what there is of it is enough. For both of them. 'I love you,' he hisses again, somewhere in the high, the sentiment emerging as naturally as escaping air, the only truth worth saying. And she answers by wrapping herself beneath him and running her hands up and down the length of his back, her palms and fingertips riding the nubs of his spine as

89

they rise and disappear, rise and then disappear. In union, their bodies feel so well met, even the parts that have lost their shape and turned soft, and there are moves they can make that still feel almighty, tricks they know of, having run these paths before.

But nothing lasts for ever.

IV

Happy Families

Books, for Caitlin, had never been anything less than a kind of sorcery. As a child she was constantly armed, and even by her late pre-teens she'd become so voracious a reader that the twice-weekly visits to her local library could barely sate her hunger. More than just educating her, books offered release and freedom in every direction. Desert islands and deepest space became as real as the Brooklyn streets; she learned of headless horsemen and river-rafting, Victorian-era London and dogs that would trek across continents to find their masters, and she got to know peg-legged pirates, pipe-smoking detectives and cowboys who drank and brawled but who loved their horses more than their women and who prized honour above all else.

And almost from the time she could lay down sentences of her own, her ambitions were clear. She'd hear often, in the years ahead, even sometimes from teachers – cardigan-clad types who'd been made bitter as limes by the directions their own lives had taken – that the likes of her didn't become writers, that her world wasn't the world of stories. But even at that young age, she knew differently, because writing was not about money and colleges and degrees but about seeing, and finding the right words, and about making sense of things. Paper was cheap – free, at her local library, at least to her, and always given with a smile, three or four pages at a time – and pens or pencils could be borrowed. And writing wasn't about being good, either; it was about doing it, and wanting to do it. Needing to. She had stories in her head, jumbles of them, and lying in bed, listening to the noises of the night-time and watching the shadows crawl across her ceiling and walls, raised from the darkness by the headlights of passing cars, she'd play them out and fantasise about the books they'd one day make.

Her earliest writing was in keeping with her age, full of angst and exaggeration, necessary in terms of foundation but otherwise worthless. Eventually, her adolescent scribbling did lose some of its romantic lustre and begin to take a serious shape, but it was only after she had broken from the giggles and tears of her childish years that her more thoughtful scatterings fell into place. The trick was making the time to look closely, at herself as well as her surroundings, and acknowledging and accepting the particular edges of emotion that were starting to break the skin, the longings and fears that had probably always existed for her on some level but which had never previously demanded attention. Feelings for and towards love, sex and all the in-between, the business of playing house, the sharing of self, the cooking, the cleaning, squeezing pennies, hustling through days. This was life, the quiet end of living that, nevertheless, had to be lived in full-blown manner. And amid the confusion of so much newness, her refuge became the nightly couple of hours spent lying face down on her bed, pouring little bits at first and then, eventually, everything of herself out onto saffron-coloured legal pads, herself in the reimagined guises of middle-aged housewives and little girls lost in forests, of soldiers fighting endless, futile wars and fishermen pinned down by demon storms. She worked longhand, using an old fountain pen, a cheap but well-meant thing gifted by somebody long since forgotten to the man she'd thought of as her stepfather, and which had been abandoned on the run for her to discover. With its tarnished chrome casing rubbed to the point of splitting and a chipped nib that functioned only when held at a particular angle, it felt heavily of near misses and squandered opportunities, yet it seemed crafted for the channels of her hand and acted as a conduit of sorts, the oracular means of getting the words down onto pages, the right words, coaxing them loose and making sense of them.

By nineteen, the age at which her writing had really begun to blossom, she and Thomas were already living together. Cohabiting, as her mother called it, and kept on calling it right up until the day she died, a word to be clung to even after it had been made obsolete by a marriage vow, as if it implied something of them both, some deep creek in their respective characters. Cohabiting: a sour-milk word to turn anyone's face, too many syllables over too short a span, too much in need of chewing. But that was Madge Healy all over and all the way through. Perhaps her mind had reworked its own past into something more presentable, or maybe it was just a generational thing, something Irish-blooded that worsened with maturity, but she, of all people, should have known better, and should have stood last in line when it came to passing judgement on others. Before her heart gave out while standing in a Brooklyn deli's lunchtime queue, barely a week shy of her fifty-sixth birthday, she'd been a short stout type, thick all over, with sagging shoulders, big heavy breasts, fat arms and a broad face made ruddy from hot kitchens, from everything dealt with at a run and from nights spent full to teeming with cheap whiskey. Her eyes had the same hard wet green of pond grass and her puncture wound of a mouth was set full of tiny grey and always gritted teeth. She cut her own hair, dressed out of thrift shops and worked too long and too hard. At home, she burned everything she'd ever tried to cook in a way other than simple boiling, and the flavours of Caitlin's childhood were those of incinerated bacon, watery potatoes and slimy, overdone cabbage.

Madge took an instant dislike to Thomas, and never approved of him in her daughter's life. He was not a man to be trusted, his hands were too cold, his eyes too steady. Liars, apparently, had such eyes. She'd found him that first night sitting on her couch, nestled close to Caitlin in a way that practically announced their intimacy. 'He's no good,' she said, after he'd gone. 'And he's got no Irish in him either. You only need look at him to know that.' It was such a stupid thing to say, on all counts, but exactly the sort of thing she would say. Beyond songs and soft accents, Irishness for her had been punches in the mouth and the kind of physical and emotional poverty broken in the end only by an unannounced desertion. She should have had her fill, but instead held to it as something godly. That night, she'd been to bingo, and a house rule had been broken. They were women alone, and couldn't risk strangers. He sat slouched down onto the small of his back with his legs outstretched and spread wide apart, and when he spoke he seemed to taste his smile, which showed him off as cocky, the sort of boy who thought too much of himself and too little always of others, even those who'd get close to him. He put his hand on Caitlin's knee and left it there, as if the gesture meant nothing, even when Madge began to stare, and he answered questions that weren't even asked of him with sounds rather than words, little dismissive hums and grunts. She'd have understood that a great deal of what she was seeing was mere swagger, the kind of falsehood braggadocio native to a particular breed of late teen, but she still had genuine reasons for disapproving of him, at least initially, reasons that maybe could be argued against but not really denied.

'He'll knock you up,' she said, after Caitlin had returned home a few nights later, a little after midnight, alone, her blouse looking rearranged around her slight body, a hot, sticky blush clinging to her cheeks. They'd been out for coffee, and split a slice of carrot cake, though he had confined most of his attentions to the butter-cream frosting. Caitlin thought it better not to admit that he liked to eat with his fingers instead of a fork or that they had shared the chore of sucking his fingers clean, right there in the café, where everyone could see. Her mother was waiting for dirt like that, evidence of flaws. Moving around the kitchen and preparing herself a sandwich of

95

cheese and pickle that she didn't even really want, she surrendered the facts of the night in a casual 'Confiteor' of shrugs and broken sentences that held only the illusion of transparency. Yes, he'd walked her home, and grudgingly, okay yes, they had kissed, in a dark part of the hallway downstairs. But it was just a kiss, hardly mortal-sin territory, and a kiss didn't make him Jack the Ripper.

The careful edit purged all mention of his attempts to coax more from her: his imploring insistence that they go on somewhere, by which he actually meant go back somewhere, back to his place, the little box room in the apartment that he shared with one of his brothers and one of his friends. He swore on his life that they'd have the room to themselves, without disturbance, but she just smiled and shook her head because no meant no but it also meant not yet. In the hallway, she let go of his hand but stood close until he kissed her, a long slow kiss that seemed a little nervous at first but gained in confidence as it built momentum, and she didn't pull away when he began to pick open some buttons but did when he tried to push for a little extra.

'He will,' her mother said, her face twisting into a mean smile. 'Mark my words. He'll knock you up, and then he'll be gone and you'll be left behind. It's happened to plenty before you.' The abruptness of the following silence caused the words to press uncomfortably against what Madge really wanted to say, but she seemed to realise that the rest was better left implied, so she clenched her mouth shut and watched, breathing in hisses through her nose, as Caitlin cut her sandwich into neat triangles and stacked them peak-side up on a small plate, just as a restaurant might.

Madge's were the natural concerns of any single mother. Love for her had always been a cold plunge, a short-lived distraction of sunshine and laughter before the inevitable wreckage on the unseen reefs. There'd been men in her own life, two in a serious way, and on both occasions she'd given up the whole of herself, to no avail. First, fleetingly, to Brian, Caitlin's blood father but a man only ever known to the child by name and by repute; and then, later, to Pete, a different kind of man, who came and, at least for a while, acted the part. The misses left her damaged at a chemical depth, and once Pete walked out she turned stony against romance, locked herself down against the creep of it. On a surface level, it seemed no great loss, because she was tough and capable. But those who saw only surfaces didn't get to know the countless nights when the low wet notes of her crying came through the wall into Caitlin's bedroom, and Caitlin, after tossing and turning and covering her head with a pillow against the intrusion, had no other option but to get up, switch on the radio and try to drown herself in music. On those nights, sometimes deep into the small hours, the holes between songs heaved with broken-hearted weeping, and the songs themselves, even the ones that jumped to seemingly happier beats, caught the taint and turned melancholic.

Her recollection of Pete is a blur of hints and imaginings. There are times when she can see his face as clearly as if he is sitting no more than five feet away, and other moments when her mind conjures only the shape of him, the ungainly and slightly apologetic manner in which he managed to fill space. His name rings occasionally through her thoughts, but it is always framed in her mother's voice, and delivered with thrust, condemning and accusatory, a straight-armed blade. Pete shared somewhere close to four years of their collective home life, stepping into the fray during the weeks leading up to Caitlin's third birthday, a tall, thin man, quiet except in drink and even then, more often than not, maudlin. On his days off he would take her by the hand and they'd walk to the end of the block to buy chocolate or ice cream or the sort of old-fashioned boiled sweets – bull's-eyes and mint humbugs and acid drops and clove rocks – that she loved mainly because he did. She felt small and safe and happy beside him, skipping along at a little half-run to keep pace with his long strides, and proud that he'd agreed or elected to be her father.

He had a great passion for baseball. He'd talk of it incessantly, in a dusty murmur that whispered air through the words and which made him sound like no one else she had ever heard. The voice seemed a penned-in thing, far too small for his frame, but it lent their time together a delicious sense of conspiracy. Most of what he had to say passed her by, but that did nothing to dampen his enthusiasm. For her, the sound of him was enough, puffing his way through the words, soft as wet dirt. Later, she'd understand that he spoke the way he did because his voice had been for generations shaped with another language in mind and that even if he'd forgotten the words or replaced them with others the essence of that different music at least remained with him, the lilt a thing ingrained. And sometimes, as they walked and just for fun, she'd sing 'Take Me Out to the Ball Game', timidly and unbidden, putting it up as backdrop to his chatter. He'd smile whenever she did that, the sort of smile she loved to see because of how it made her feel. His eyes would pinch a little as his mouth fell open, and she knew even at five or six that if she were ever to see him cry it would be with an expression that matched this exactly, adding only tears to the equation.

She finds it difficult even now to imagine the gravitational pull that must have existed between him and Madge. Perhaps especially now, given the perspective of time. But love is a language that often defies translation. Pete was not handsome. He had a very long face, slender and flat, with too much forehead on show and too much chin. His bones came very close to the surface, yellowing his skin where they ridged or cornered. He worked in the subway, some type of construction or laborious maintenance duty that kept to an odd rolling shift arrangement as dictated by train schedules, so time was a watery thing for him, with nights running ever into days. Any sort of natural light must have felt like an otherworldly treat. At Madge's insistence, and just to keep the illusion of a family life, they often ate porridge breakfasts at midnight and dinner at ten a.m., overcooked cabbage, turnip or sprouts, potatoes that fell out of their skins and turned to powder on the plate, stringy corned beef or offal meat, heart or kidneys or liver, cubed into chunks and fried to a crunch. He'd eat as though there was tax to be paid on leftovers, the way men fresh out of prison often eat, getting the food down with assisting gulps of stout if it happened to be anywhere close to pay day and with buttermilk if they were all spent up on good things for the week.

Perhaps because of its limited exposure to sunlight, his flesh was pallid except for the insomniac bruises that underscored his small pale eyes. Sometimes, if the weather was hot and they were going for ice cream, he'd take off his cheap suit jacket and hold it by a thumb over his shoulder as they walked, and in those moments another side of him revealed itself, allowing Caitlin a telling glimpse of the footloose man capable on the least whim of hitching his way clean across the country, the type who could easily go a month without shaving, sleep in fields or under bridges, and who could fight without qualm, equally well with fists or with something broken and jagged, for his supper. At his best, he was a good man, the times when he was able to keep a distance between himself and anything harder than beer; and those must have been the moments that held Madge enthralled, even if she was strict with him about everything, about getting home an hour late, not taking out the garbage or leaving his dirty socks beneath the bed. When she went at him he simply bowed his head and took it, though if he was within reach of whiskey then things could go either way. Caitlin remembers mornings, not many but a few, when Madge could only talk in croaks and from behind a staunching towel or handkerchief, but she also recalls a night awakening to peculiar birdlike whines and finding her mother lying face down on the bed with the hem of her nightgown tugged most of the way up her back while Pete, upright and completely naked, bucked against her from behind, his hands kneading and gathering loose fistfuls of her flabby sides, luxuriating in that swell. The details remain vivid for Caitlin, the sight of their bodies shining like exposed bone, and that wall of small sound: the relentless slap of flesh, the jerking breaths, the choked, misshapen words and half-words, and more than anything else the absurd delicacy of the squeals knocked loose from Madge with every taken thrust, animal sobs immediately amplified by the darkness, in intensity if not in actual volume.

Was it love? Well, who but the involved could ever truly know? What's clear is that, for four years, Pete was there, as a father, husband and provider. Talking baseball, dozing off at the morning table after a long night spent in the tunnels, but tossing and turning in bed, kicking loose of the sheets, getting up to open the window, to close the window, to drink water, to soak a facecloth against the stinking Brooklyn summers before finally, around noon, just giving up and taking himself down to the corner bar or, if he was out of credit, to the building's front stoop, where he'd settle on the top step, prop himself against the jamb of the open doorway and catnap between passing chats. Living that way wasn't easy, but they got by, and while his appetites stayed small there was a lot of room for laughter in their lives.

Then one day he was simply gone. Caitlin still thinks about it sometimes, when she is alone. A day in late summer, the golden air burned and thickening to redness with the shadows of early evening. Out on the street some kids had opened a fire hydrant and were taking turns leaping through its spouting arc, shrieking against the

101

breathtaking coldness of the water. The pavement gleamed and the men out on the stoops in their shirtsleeves or undershirts watched and smiled and shook their heads and talked about how it had been back when they themselves were kids.

By six, mother and child were at the table. Madge said nothing, just sat there in a pale blue sleeveless blouse that bloomed navy around the armpits. A gloss of sweat lathered her temples and now and again a bead would gather and then break in a quick runnel down her cheek. Dinner was cold cuts and a simple salad, and at first she insisted that they wait for Pete but after a while, twenty minutes, half an hour, she relented and let Caitlin eat. Her own plate, though, remained untouched. She sat there, waiting, thinking bad thoughts and then worse ones. When the heat became too much for her she unbuttoned her blouse and let it hang open. Her great breasts bulged inside the drab white cups of her bra and her skin had reddened in places, prickling with rash. She was still there an hour later, when the daylight at last began to dim.

Over the years, newspapers have printed countless stories of men going out for packs of cigarettes and staying gone. As a statement of intent there are few as effective. There is even a word for it, desertion, the sort of word that feels like grit on your tongue and makes you want to spit, or at least wince, upon speaking it. Caitlin stood by the window in the last of the sun, and again in the days after, gazing out onto the street and waiting for a glimpse of something familiar. She sensed that their lives had turned to pulp but was too young to understand the magnitude of what had happened. She can't recall ever crying about his leaving, but she does remember an overwhelming feeling of displacement, as if somehow the heart had dropped from its perch inside her body, leaving behind a high and gaping cavity. The oddness of that sensation lingered with her a long time and maybe, in some way, lingers still.

Talking was never part of the equation. While the wound was still fresh, and careful to avoid collisions, she knew better than to try; but even later, growing up, her attempts at broaching the subject were always met with a kind of reactionary paralysis. Madge possessed an entire neighbourhood of rage, but the merest mention of Pete would turn her instantly to glass. It was understandable. People defend themselves in different ways. Some can talk openly about the bad side of the world, some will shout or sing about it and a few will even turn it into great art. Madge's way was to work a kind of reverse transubstantiation, some alchemical fast-hand Monte trick that morphed flesh and blood into merest matter. Even in absentia, Pete retained a bedrock permanence in their lives, but she'd stare back hard at any challenge, refusing to speak, and her denial had the gradual effect of eroding away his essence. This locked-down state was her mode of self-preservation, the tool or weapon that helped her to endure what for her had been a thing of total ruin. And without the details, Caitlin could no more than speculate as to what exactly had gone bad.

Most likely, some argument had triggered his walking out, because there was always something going on and rows seemed to seep one into the next with them. Over drink, over some act of selfishness, over God alone knew what. But why that particular row should have been any more ferocious than the thousand others opened up the floor to all manner of fancy. Was it something said that could never be taken back, a thing so foul it did not bear remembering? Was it something done? Or was there, this time, perhaps someone else involved, another woman, offering him more, offering escape, even love? Was that what made this fight so different and so definitive? Maybe. Caitlin wondered, calculated the possibilities, indulged the variables. But it was a futile practice. And the passing of years have done nothing to clarify the situation. Even now, all she knows for certain is that Pete was there the way that the walls of their apartment were, as solid and assured, as dependable; talking baseball, smelling sour, looking always washed-out, always more than slightly sad, a tall, thin, slack-shouldered man with big hands that never seemed quite comfortable or at rest. And then, without a word of explanation or even a kiss goodbye, he was gone. As to whether or not he'd been in contact since, there was no way of knowing. It's possible that he called, or wrote, because total abandonment didn't fit with what Caitlin thought she understood of his nature, and a spoken or written word might help to explain the tears that came to mark the worst of their night-times. But if letters had made it through then they did not survive. Nothing did, except the memories.

Love complicated matters. For Caitlin, meeting Thomas added a certain volatility to the world. She liked him, right from the beginning, liked the way he looked in his tight black denims and with his shirtsleeves rolled high towards his shoulders. And even more than that, how he looked at her, with a hungered gaze that stuck like thrown mud. He wasn't a troublemaker, and had no involvement in gangs or drugs, but being with him made her feel as if she were bending some law. Sometimes, when they were out together, he'd lean her up against a wall and just stare, eating into her with his wide dark eyes. Silence was easy then, in a way that it never would be later on, but at that stage, with everything still sweetness, a gaze said more than enough. He'd put her gently against the wall, bring himself close in and stare until she became entranced, and even as he began to kiss her mouth his hands would be going for her breasts, through her shirt or sweater but even so, fearless and unashamed, right there on the street, in public. Later, deep into the night, she'd lie in her bed and relive it all, trying to reawaken the sense of life he'd given her, and after a while she decided that she liked him for many reasons but she liked him most of all for the innocence of who he was trying to be. And it was easy to fall into his game, to catch a little of his swagger, and to convince herself that what she was feeling for him could in fact be the real thing.

By the end of their first year as a couple, they'd taken a shabby two-room apartment in Hudson Heights. Breathing one another's air was a new challenge but, with the bloom of what they had going still then rich and ripe, the equilibrium could hold. And Thomas, being from a big family and suited to confinement, moved like a dancer. That was the trick, he said. That was how to navigate the dark. Back then, he was very good at romance, at the notion of it. He held her hand at unexpected moments and kissing thrilled him because it led them towards such heightened states. She learned things about him, emotionally as well as physically, things that made sense of certain aspects but which threw others out of focus. And she supposed that he learned quite a bit about her too, even though she was slow with revelations that felt too intrusive.

In bed, those first months, he was incessant. They took turns devouring one another; even in sleep their flesh seemed to answer some addiction or magnetic inclination, separate from thought or consequence. She felt happy then, and she smiled a lot, from a deep place, because his enthusiasm was catching. But a piece of her remained untouchable.

Of course, Madge disapproved. Time had proven her correct on some matters and dead wrong on others, though being privy to very little in the way of actual detail her prejudices remained steadfast. As far as she was concerned, Thomas was trouble waiting to happen, and what he and her daughter were doing, shacking up together, was nothing less than sinful. She couldn't have known how often the subject of marriage infiltrated the young lovers' conversations, almost always at Thomas's prompting, a dialogue not merely confined to intimate moments, when the blood was up and things got said, but one that was actual and ongoing and which found itself unfurled at every opportunity, over breakfast, over coffee, over beer, always considering, weighing the pros and cons of the wedded state. A few months in, they'd had a close call on a pregnancy, but Caitlin miscarried. It came and went, without great trauma, because she'd barely even been pregnant at all, only a few weeks along. Thomas was there when it happened, and he'd taken her into the bathroom, peeled off her clothes, stood her in the bathtub and washed her, and neither one of them had even cried, though it did feel as if tears were due, or owed. They'd have plenty of time for this, he told her, then and again later on. And maybe it was for the best. Caitlin smiled for him and wasn't at all surprised at how truthful the words felt. It was not that she didn't want children, because she did, or that he didn't, because he most definitely did; it was just that neither one of them felt ready yet for kids, not when so much was still at such an uncertain stage between them.

By that time, she'd become serious about her writing. It had always been a part of her, but now she began to believe that it was something to which she could commit herself, happily, for the rest of her life. It meant giving over hours every day to the frustration of building and unravelling sentences, filling up pages and breaking them back down, trying to make some sense of the things she thought about. But when it ran well, when she caught the music inside the words, something moved through her and everything lightened, or seemed to click into focus. It never lasted, but was a state worth chasing. The things she wrote at this point were the things she needed to write. At that age, eighteen, nineteen, her ambitions tended to outreach her abilities, but the constant falling short was in itself a kind of achievement. She'd heard or read Beckett's words on failure and held to them, and she refused to go easy. Nothing was beyond the pale, and no hurt too delicate. She thought about Thomas and what they had together, who he was beyond who he pretended to be, and where he was going, where he'd end up. And she thought about the past that Madge had lived, the sufferings and sacrifices that might have accounted for so much bitterness. She taught herself to look and watch and really see, and she tried hard to empathise. Missing the mark, more often than not, but occasionally uncovering something of worth, some revelatory moment. But when it came to Pete, her way felt blocked. With him, all she had were memories, and probably half-imagined ones at that. He was dark shadows, a ghost, a feature of her heavy childhood afternoons ripe with the smell of tar and sweet things, smiling through the traffic noise at music spilling from some unseen radio; and part, too, of the moments of war, just sitting there, eyes half closed, mouth clenched, while her mother stood above him, screaming like a cat.

And then, one night, another memory came through, long forgotten and just as dreamlike as the rest but as real, too, once it hit the air, of the morning when, in a drunken state, he had taken her onto his lap and put his hand down inside her pyjama bottoms. He'd come off the ugly shift, ten to six, and afterwards had hit a bar with a couple of his workmates, and he was always at his worst when he drank his way into a day. Her mother had just stepped out for eggs and was gone maybe five minutes, and there'd been nothing more to it than that, but touching was still a long way over the line. She didn't think she'd cried, but couldn't be sure, and she wondered whether or not she'd felt afraid. She'd have understood, of course, even without the need for Madge's repeated warnings, that nobody had permission to touch her there, but she was six years old, and at that age, especially back then, the rules were set. At six, you spoke only when spoken to, you never answered back, you came when called, and more than anything else you trusted a parent, body and soul.

From his slouched position in the centre of the settee, he called her to him and settled her side-saddle on his lap, held her there with one gentle hand on her shoulder, his eyes closed with all the calmness of sleep and his face for once serene, breathing long slow breaths that whistled through his nose, tipping into pitch just as they reached their end, before the vacuous reversal. And all she did was keep still, uncertain at first, then nervous, while his touch without explanation pressed coldly against her belly and then inside the elastic waistband of her pyjama bottoms and lower down, between her legs. Maybe needing to shift the focus of her attention, she studied his face, let herself become fascinated by the little network of creases fanning in talons from the corners of his eyes and the way the pores of his cheeks lay open and cratered with dirt, with the soot that he had brought up with him from the city's depths. She might have cried out when his touch hardened, but her voice would have retained its nightingale pitch and that part of it was over very quickly, probably because he was cautious of being caught out by a scream or by causing a bleed. He sat there like that, perfectly still, with his fingers tucked into her lap and a look of shut-down contentment on his face, and he took his hand back only when Madge announced herself in the hallway, talking aloud to no one in particular about traffic even at this hour or about how in Christ's

109

name the day could get so hot so early. Stopped as if he was simply tired of the game, or bored by it. His eyes remained closed and there was nothing to be seen in his face, no joy, no fear, nothing.

As the door swung open, Caitlin slipped from his lap and hurried off to the bathroom, and this was something worth writing about too, something to be explored, the sense that, even at such a precocious age, she'd felt the need to hide what had just occurred, as if the wrong-doing was in some way down to her. Was this proof that guilt was an instinctive response rather than a social infliction, or was it that even at five or six years old she was sensitive to the precarious state of their family's balance, to the fact that sides would have to be taken in such a feud and that there were no absolute guarantees as to how things would play out? She stood in the bathroom for a long time, with the door to her back closed but not locked, facing the window and caged in that white space, trying to decide if there was anything to be gained by crying. For something to do, and because the silence bothered her, she turned on the basin's cold tap and let the water run. Her heart was beating hard. Everything felt out of place, though in the mirror above the sink she looked the same as always. A dime-sized crust of scab set her features at an imbalance, the result of a fall in the street a week or two before, a clumsy trip taken while chasing down a ball or skipping out a game of hopscotch. She'd cried over that, even though it hadn't really hurt too badly, not once the initial sting of the impact began to fade, and she had climbed up onto Pete's lap then, too. But that evening there'd been no drink, and he'd held her to his chest and rocked her gently, just as any father would, whispering sympathy until her tears subsided and the rags of her breath turned smooth again. Once she quieted, he set her back on her feet, drew her close and, in a gentle way, with nothing but love involved, kissed her wounded cheek. It wasn't a deep cut, there was no need for a stitch. 'It'll be better before you're married,' he said, and she furrowed her brow and asked him, still feigning a pout, if that was a promise because what if she should decide to get married tomorrow? A week or two weeks on, the scab was still there, skewing her image in the mirror, and traces of it remained even into the next year, marring the photographs taken on the morning of her first Holy Communion, a penny's worth of pink pebbledash the only blemish to her otherwise angelic beauty. A few of those pictures still survive, and the best of them shows her standing in the church doorway, head and shoulders in the shot, seven years old, her hair done in darkish reams beneath the gauzy bunching of a thrown-back veil, her hands tiny and pressed palms-together in prayer to just beneath her chin. She looks sweet, but for some reason not quite innocent. The pink mark catches the eye, but it is also impossible to ignore the fact that she is not smiling for the camera.

Once she began examining her life to such a degree, a new intimacy entered her writing. Her fiction took on a realism that it had not previously possessed, and real meant all the edges, all the ugly scenes, the boredom, tantrums and horror shows as well as the moments of beauty. In short, the kind of words that once said stayed said. And her process actually benefited from the accepting of someone else into her life-space, the sharing of things, food, laughter, a bed, bodies. It was a new kind of nakedness, thick with dread and exhilaration, and its freshness caused the world to crackle and spit. Energy sang from every surface and everything about her days and nights felt inspired.

Their financial situation took time to stabilise, but Thomas had a head for money and a talent for handling it. Initially, they'd had to drag hard to keep a stride ahead of obese tabs and rent that had too easily slipped a week or a month overdue, but by his careful and often creative cash-management techniques, and by putting the occasional bit of shoulder into it, he managed to keep even the most threadbare of ends together. Work-wise, he kicked like a chained bull in a bog to ensure they remained afloat, and he could do in a joyful way at twenty-two what he'd struggle to manage at forty. In business matters he was cold as tombstone, and he hustled his wares to friends of friends and to the sort of flooded-basement companies that needed to cut every corner in the ledger and to squeeze those cents to shrapnel without paying anything even approaching the going rate, because twenty-two years old was an age still coated in the skin and brawn of youth, and at that age a brain for figures and a shake of salt in the bloodstream felt like more than enough, it felt like plenty. Back then, there were all sorts of names for that, balls being about the best of them, but the trick was to keep the faith in that imminent break without daring to go hunting too hard for the horizons.

Even when the mire seemed set to swallow them up, his self-belief, and his refusal to take no for an answer, kept them alive. And a change was coming. After several months spent bludgeoning the hotshot accountancy firm of Kinsey, Morgan and Davenport with enough beefed-up résumés to commemorate a small forest, he finally succeeded in breaking their will and got himself on the payroll, conditional on him finishing out his part-time community college degree, at the nickel-and-dime level of dogsbody numbers-cruncher. It was the pay-off for a life of stubborn persistence, very much at the asshole end of things, but a step on the stairs and a glimpse at the heady glimmer of faraway stars. And, most importantly, it gave them a small, steady influx of money in the bank, first of the month every month, guaranteed. For a couple so used to pressing the print off pennies, this new-found security was a wonder. The days took on a lightness they'd never previously possessed, and the nights turned soft and blue. He'd arrive home a little after six, or on school nights after ten, to find Caitlin waiting, ready with kisses that earned their smile, and they'd sit and eat dinner, chat about work and traffic and the hundred other things that cluttered up a shift in the city. It was a game of house, and they played like children, knowing their roles, acting grown up, but really only feeding the myth and filling a shared void. And when they gave in to what felt like the natural progression and set about finally tying the knot, that was something of a game, too. The formalities kept to a suggestive level, but Thomas was the first man to ever lay the chance of marriage before her, the first to show that or any kind of interest, and even if

113

the magnitude of his commitment probably wasn't everything it might have been, refusal didn't feel like an option. At twenty years old, she could see no one else crowding her future, and incredible though it would come to seem from a later vantage, at that age dread held a significant amount of sway in her decision. Marriage, beyond the colouring of love in all its wild and gory splash, was a deal struck, a thing of give and take, of opening her legs when she didn't particularly feel like it as well as when she did and of working to fulfil her half of perfecting a life together, or if perfect proved too high an aim then at least settling for bearable. He'd look after her, and she'd do her best by him. And in between, she'd find happiness in words. As a notion it was all clean air.

During her childhood years, back when her mother was at it with both hands and Pete bounced sullenly between drunken states, Caitlin had spent thought like free money on how marriage would be. The unspeakable had only happened once, but ever after, even beyond the day when Pete did not return home, she felt herself braced against more of it. Marriage was a mind-escape, and consisted on that fantasy level of smiling to beat the band, baking cakes and cookies, and kissing in the dark. It was dining out on candlelit nights and holding hands whenever the opportunity offered itself, and it was the pure happiness of having someone who would protect and cherish her, who'd lay down his life for her, if needs be, without a heartbeat of hesitation. Growing up withered most of her delusions, but at twenty, even after two going on for three years of togetherness through thin and thinner, a little of the dreamy stuff lingered. And love or less, the trump card that marriage held, at least in her estimation, was the clear-heeled escape from the dread possibility of a life lived alone.

In and out of the marriage, the writing flowed. She welcomed a lot of mornings from her place at the kitchen table, facing the window and perched above her page, wrapped in an old flannel nightgown and with her second or third helping of strong black French roast cooling in its mug, and more than once she'd stolen from bed with the clock only just the wrong side of midnight, alive and wide awake with the aftermath flush of lovemaking. The writing then was in the thinking and the forging. She wandered blindly, fighting frustration, finding her way by touch and sheer will, until stories formed. Yet once done, the results often panicked her. What she was doing didn't in her mind equate with what other writers, real writers, were doing. To her, writers, the ones whose work earned them the title, remained essentially mythical creatures, names that seemed to evoke images and worlds in themselves. Hemingway, Steinbeck, Mailer, Updike, Nabokov were, to her, fictions forging fiction. These were not the names of anyone she'd ever met, and they were not a part of her landscape. Their processes and hers might have shared some elements, but the sentences they sculpted were full of musical assurance, humming and crackling with all the electricity of life. It was inconceivable to her that they could know anything of the fumbling desperation she suffered a draft or even five drafts into a story. Their words danced; hers lay comatose. She slaved over her stories, but there were entire weeks when her efforts at resuscitation raised only twitches. Writing, at that point, had become so much a part of her identity that stopping was not yet a viable option, and what kept her going was the realisation that she at least got to set her own rules, and that no one had to see the finished work if she did not feel comfortable about showing it. But it did little to soften her sense of inadequacy.

She'd been nine weeks married when 'Foreign Affairs', the first truly worthwhile thing she had written, was plucked from the slush pile at one of the mid-level national journals and pressed into print. By then, she'd already been through the shredder with the story, had suffered a good ten or a dozen form-letter rejections of the kind that can ball up your confidence and bin it like tossed paper, to the point where all faith in her own judgement had long since been worn away. She took the phone call with her arms coated to both elbows in the soapsuds of the evening's washing-up. A man's voice, dispassionate and cluttered with the distractions of other chores, each far more important to his day than she was, introduced himself and informed her, in a way that could never have passed for a request, of his journal's interest in publishing her story, as long as she would agree to a minor edit in the second paragraph of page three and a couple of clarifying points elsewhere. She whispered her grateful replies in half-speed monosyllables, and after settling the phone's receiver back in its cradle slumped to the floor and cried, without really knowing why. Thomas, thinking that something was wrong, got up from his chair in front of a ball game, lifted her to her feet and took her in his arms. Between sobs, she explained what had just happened, and he smiled and congratulated her even as his hand worked its way inside her blouse and began thumbnailing her left nipple to stiffness.

The success was minuscule, a pittance stipend and a few complimentary copies of the journal, but as a validation for her years of discipline and hard work, it felt immense. That evening she and Thomas celebrated with a five-dollar bottle of red wine and afterwards loved their way to sleep. And lying there in the clammy, post-coital darkness, with her husband face down beyond the blankets, and the bedside radio tuned low and soft to a west-coast ball game, she dared finally to entertain the notion of a career in writing. The things she thought about were wild, but in her mind, spinning as it was, hit all the corners. And in the weeks and months that followed, she set about making these imaginings reality, applying herself to the task with great discipline, approaching it as actual work, setting herself targets, daily word-count goals that she hardly ever met but which at least kept her focused and moving in a good direction. When 'Foreign Affairs' arrived in published form she held the journal in her hands as something precious, then sat at the kitchen table and feasted on its contents, reading it thoroughly from start to finish, every-thing apart from her own story, which she bypassed after a cursory bounce-through, not wanting its failings to sap the good from such a pleasurable moment. Even seeing her name in print had unexpectedly proven a cause of both anxiety and exhilaration: the latter because she happened to be sharing page space with some recognisable names, including a Pulitzer Prize-winning poet; the former because her story had opened up, albeit in thickly veiled fashion, such a piece of her own life for all the world to see. The names had been changed to shelter the guilty, and even people who knew her well would have needed to look closely in order to make the connections, but she knew. During the story's writing she'd given no thought at all as to how it would be perceived, especially as it pertained to her, to the life she'd lived, and she consoled herself with the assurance that this was what writers did, that it was what Faulkner did, and Flannery O'Connor and Hemingway, and so on. They wrote what they knew and what they cared about. She closed her eyes and decided not to feel ashamed for following their lead.

Her advance moved at a snail's crawl. Every day, she found an hour or two, sometimes more, for the page. She started no fires, and challenged herself only within the work, but by the time she'd reached her mid-twenties, that dreamed-of future seemed possible. There'd been disappointments, stories so intrinsically broken that they couldn't be made to work no matter how much time and effort she committed to them, and even the few stories that did click had to survive tides of rejection before washing up on some agreeable shore, but the small successes kept her alive. Her sixth published story even earned her a small award, a piece of glass and a modest cheque, as well as inclusion in a year's-best anthology, and this in turn brought letters of casual enquiry from three well-known literary agencies. She felt comfortable within the scale of a story and enjoyed the illusion of control, but a part of her had begun to crave a bigger canvas. Already, she was several months and probably fifty salvageable pages along on a short novel still keeping up the pretence of being a long story, work that she couldn't yet bring herself to even speak about much less show to anyone but which had her bristling at the gills with the sheer joy of getting the words down.

By then, Michael had become a fixture in her world. They'd met in a bar some three years earlier, an accident of fate. Glances that became stuck, the exchange of smiles, the shift in her breathing; the way it happens the world over. The hole inside her hadn't even been apparent until he set about filling it. He was with his cousin, and a bottle above his limit by the time they got around to talking, and even though it was he who approached her she played a part in leading him on. From the beginning, they both had the score down pat. Neither one of them was free and available, neither one had been out hunting a fix. But something clicked. She could feel the gears grinding, clock-work pieces bolting into place. The moment had that sort of deep physicality. And from there, it was almost easy. Resistance was minimal, and futile, because beauty really does lurk within the beholding eye. It would have been easy as sucking air to walk away. A quick shake of the head and that would have been that, a flirt, a drink and a full stop to finish the sentence. But when he asked her to dance she gave him her hand. Just like people do on the big screen. Hesitant, but only for effect, counting out the seconds and letting him hang, then raising herself to him, wrist bent for him to take. And even drunk, or even on the way to that, he knew on just the right instinctive level how this worked, gripping her daintily by the fingers but firmly at the hip once they found themselves a square of space out on the floor. They came together with the kind of bang heard or felt by no one else but them, and they moved clumsily, dodging rather than floating between tables, their connective style absolutely devoid of rhythm, their bodies separate from the beat of the music but not from one another. Talk felt out of place, but there was a cogency about their interactions. They danced, if what they were doing could at all be classed as dancing, and when it felt right to do so she lay her face against his shoulder and smelled the day he'd just put in, the long mean hours spent tucked beneath the hood of some heap. Greased and oiled, heavy to beyond exhaustion with sweat that fell shy of blood only by its colour and its reek. His night- and day-long stubble burned her cheekbone and temple, yet she returned for that sensation over and over, pressing to feel it and nestling so that his mouth would fall beside her ear, and sometimes, as they moved into a turn, against it, and his breath scorched a kind of fever into her then so that it took all she had to keep from grinding herself against his thigh.

That night, everything changed. The stars, rare and irresistible, with all their predestined alignments, fell into view. Alcohol excused some things but could not explain how being with him made her feel. It wasn't that she didn't love her husband, she told herself, and told Michael, the first time they'd slept together. Thomas had a kind of detached goodness. He worked hard for them, for their home, the things they needed. He was safe and loyal and not too demanding. He'd speak of love only occasionally, and only ever in gasps, always with his eyes clenched and maybe his heart clenched, too, as if it were somehow causing him pain. Out on the street or in the subway, turned out in a halfway-good suit and carrying a chrome and black leatherette briefcase, he always seemed so assured, able, even daring. In fact, he was a man of small, manageable ambitions. He talked a lot about reality but lived life a level beneath it, threading only where the bombs could never fall. A lot of men are that way, and a lot of women need that. Sometimes, she herself needed it. But need and want are different things. She loved him and she knew that he loved her, in as much as he was capable of loving anyone, though there was a lot he would not do for that love, and a lot she wouldn't do either. She loved him but he never made her ache for him. And at her age, twenty-two years old, with so much just beginning to slip into place and so much of the world opening up for her, she was finding that she needed more out of life. Love had, for the first time, revealed its shades of intent.

She felt no pride in her selfishness. And even if what she and Michael were doing was more than merely selfish then that was still how she saw it. Then and still. Even with other elements factored in, and even after years of trawling for new angles of reasoning.

The first full day she and Michael spent together, she had undressed from deep within a trance. The drinking and dancing were part of the night before, and Michael, perhaps sensing the magnitude of her fragility, was gentle. He held her beside the bed and they kissed standing up, with a depth of concentration, slowly conquering their initial terror. The curtains were drawn so that their naked-ness could feel easy, but it was a morning still shy of noon in late summer and the sun was blazing, and the pleated off-white polyester was too thin to make any kind of stoppable difference to the impact of the day. He kissed her mouth and then her neck, taking his time, studying her face on one side from the centre of her chin to the small tight lobe of her ear, because it was all new, every taste and texture. Between connections, the whispered press of his breath lay hot on her skin against the wetness he'd caused, and he returned again and again to her right ear and was careful with it, following the whorls of cartilage with the point of his tongue, taking its rim, its lobe between his teeth, pinching little dimples into its pulpy flesh. She could feel his fascination as a thing of genuine wonder, even awe, and it made her smile. And while his mouth worked with passion, his hands were far more considerate, caressing and savouring her small breasts, tracing a swathe down over her ribcage to her hips. Educating himself to every nuance of a body still at that age good for long miles. When he moved her to the bed and stood a moment over her, appetite brightening his face as she lay down, she stretched out and, so suddenly exposed, shuddered with a shock of fear and excitement. Her breath felt slight inside her, reedy in her throat, like whispered laughter.

That first time had the sense of something sacred. Their bodies were freshly discovered landscapes, lush with ridges and undulations, dense from inch to inch with secrets. She clasped him in a kind of half-embrace as he bored against her, and she found his flesh slick and smooth as wet glass when her hands ran down into the sweep at the small of his back. She mouthed her love somewhere in the midst of things, but he waited until he had crawled clear of her and lay exhausted at her side. So that it would mean more and so that they had only open ground between them. There was nothing like it, and he said as much, sighing the words long and soft in the shattered aftermath. Stunned to staring, having been knocked whole seconds out of sync with the world. And she stared too, and smiled, believing him, recognising the absolute quality of his truth. The room sweltered, and in the tamped light her skin shone with his sweat and her own and her eyes sparkled silver.

Yet as precious as they might have been, it wasn't just the collisions that mattered. When apart, they each felt famished for the other, for the details of one another's existence, and on the days they came together, even the smallest morsels of revelation were savoured. He told her about his job and the ups and downs of selling, and she spoke of her writing and the things she hoped, one day, to achieve. Not awards or prizes or great wealth, but in terms of work. She had ideas, and ambition. He didn't. His job was becoming more and more a torment, but work paid the bills, and ensured survival. And where he came from, that mattered above all else. Until he met her, he was the living dead, and the only time he wanted to be himself instead of someone else, anyone else, was when she stepped into his day. Then, magic happened. As if they were sixteen again, they discussed their tastes in music, books, films, food, their favourite everything, colour, smell, places to see, time of day, time of year. Because they'd agreed right from the beginning not to look forward or to make plans that couldn't be kept, their pasts felt emphasised. While walking the pier, especially during the fine months of late spring and summer, Caitlin would often recall the Coney Island of her childhood and teens, the times when she persuaded Madge, or Madge and Pete, to bring her out, or when, later, she came in the company of friends from school. She'd remember aloud the heat, the pickle-and-mustard sweetness of the hot dogs, the music, the noise, the screams and laughter of the crowds. The happiness. Michael would hold her hand and smile, trying to imagine how it must have been, and what she'd been like, so young in the sunshine, splashing around in the cold lit water, building castles in the sand and running just to run. His own past felt so much further removed, which gave the sharing a greater intimacy, and he'd wait until they were locked safely in some room and the world was simply them before opening up. She'd lie in his arms or with her cheek against his chest when he talked about Ireland, and his island, Inishbofin, such a world away from here that it might never have existed at all outside of dreams but in fact was there still in its details whenever he reached out for it. Inishbofin, a crop of land caught hard and stubborn as a nutshell somewhere in between the folds of open sea and huge, relentless sky, and the place he still knew better than anywhere else on earth, despite his years apart from it and the manner of his leaving. Because of the restless light, a place of uncertain colour, not just the expected shades of grass or water but reds and yellows and all sorts of inlaid others, smears running one into the next like something escaped from a frame, scarring the scene in wild hillside tartan. Every time he spoke, a new suggestion made the surface, a detail long forgotten, inconsequential in itself except that it had happened, and that it belonged to him.

Speaking like this gave their silences an astonishing weight, because neither one of them had ever been so willingly undone. They'd look at one another with embarrassment, and with gratitude, for telling and listening, and for each wanting so much those pieces of the other's life.

When together, they felt absolutely right, but the empty spaces between held a lot of room for questions. Caitlin liked to indulge negative fantasies, finding something delicious in that suffering, as if by telling herself lies she could somehow heighten the truth, and she enjoyed the stab of guilt when, maybe during their next date, Michael would pass some remark, or make some small gesture, that couldn't fail to clarify his feelings. Like the day he produced a copy of the journal that had just issued her most recent story, 'Reserves', her fourth published work, and holding up a cheap ballpoint pen asked her to autograph it for him. She had already received a copy by mail, but the thrill of being presented with it so unexpectedly, and in such an alien setting, was immense. That he'd gone to the effort of actually tracking her work made her want to cry. She rolled naked onto her stomach, leafed through the journal and admired again the fine heavy-grade paper, elegant font choice and cover design. She found her own story about a third of the way in and read a few sentences from a random paragraph, seeking the tune of their music.

He wore a zebra-patterned zoot suit and burgundy-colored stove-pipe hat even on his days off, boasted a permanent gap-toothed grin, and spoke a lot about what was important and what was not. He himself was Canadian born, he said, twisting the waxed handlebars of a long drooping mustache in some imagined time to the words. He had grown up in a small, cold town in the mountains, and his ancestry was a succulent melting pot of Irish, French and Scots, spiced with delicate infusions of Ojibwa and Cree.

Taken without context, these were the words of a stranger. She remembered writing them, and rewriting them, working them for pace and rhythm, but dislocated from their plot line they did not feel part of her. Yet there was pleasure in knowing that she had written them, and that Michael had cared enough to seek them out. He lay beside her, teasing a hand over her body, allowing his touch to linger along the backs and insides of her thighs, and again at the swell of her ass. He seemed hypnotised by what he was doing, which made her smile and then laugh. She thumbed in a leisurely fashion through the journal, then with an exaggerated seriousness reached for the pen and hurried her signature onto the white space above the story's title. Autographs were something new to her. As a child she had filled the back pages of school workbooks with efforts at her signature, veering, frequently in a single attempt, between delicate spools and great florid sweeps, working always and ever towards illegibility, the generally accepted criteria for a truly impressive mark. But that was a long time ago, before cowardice set in. What she put on the page now was far more measured: To Michael, the best always, Caitlin ——. Simple and aloof, but implying more to a knowing eye. He took the journal and happily read what she had written, understanding without need for explanation, then thanked her with the sort of kiss that can't tell lies.

Almost from the beginning, she knew this for what it was. Michael let her feel; with him, she existed at a different height. The sex was part of the reason, but so was the way he'd look at her, with a bite of his lip pinched between his teeth and his stone-blue eyes transfixed, and how they were with one another, walking the pier, especially in summertime, swapping small talk, taking turns chewing on shared hot dogs or slices of pizza, certain without ever saying as much that they'd live for ever, and that they'd always be this happy. Once, out on the boardwalk, her shoelace had come undone, causing her to stumble against him. He'd caught her, then stooped to tie the lace. She tousled his hair, and while still on his knee he took her hand in both of his and offered a pleading proposal. Passers-by stopped and applauded her impassioned affirmative, and cheered the following embrace, assuming in their innocence that what they were witnessing was real. Michael laughed and kissed her, and for those few seconds she believed too, because promises become lies only when they fall short of their intention, and that day neither one of them had ever felt so young, or so happy or full of life. For those seconds of a summer's afternoon, easy in one another's arms, they were entirely who they wanted and needed to be.

Sometimes it seems unclear which of her two lives is the greater reality. Once she has slipped back into her homely skin, the afternoons spent with Michael, heightened by their rationing, take on the sensations of a dream. Against their memory, the world feels staid, and empty.

She floats through her days, her mind lacking focus. The sight of Thomas awakens her guilt, but in a pleasurable way, and she often indulges in fantasies of confession, playing it out as it might one day happen, even knowing that it never will. Dropping the news over dinner, maybe, trying to soften the bombshell to merely atomic level with just the right tone of contrition and, in an effort to avoid potential tragedy, putting nothing with bones on the plate, favouring instead the bulk comfort of a mutton stew or spaghetti bolognese, soft dense food that demands deep breaths and wholehearted endeavour. Or, if the kitchen table should feel too exposed for such revelation, targeting those few still minutes in bed after the alarm has rung them back to life, to inform him that they are lost to one another. Telling him what he surely already knows but putting it all into words so that there can be no further room for denial. A clearing of the throat, and a whisper, 'I've met someone else,' filling the holes left by dreams. Adding that she is sorry, as the silence turns blue, needing that said, even while each word from her mouth wrecks him like an axe wound. Because she is sorry, and always will be, though only for causing him hurt. She doesn't have it in her to be sorry for the rest, because that's to do with need. Her heart has earned its coldness. And in her fantasy she lies there beside him, not oblivious to his pain but out of determination untouched by it, focusing mainly on the tide of her own breath and waiting for the moment when she'll have to look up, just to know for certain that her words have impacted and, if they have, to witness the full clout of his anguish.

For a long time, leaving actually seemed possible. But the opportunities that arrived didn't linger. She knew what to say, but couldn't speak the words. And she suffered. The facts were less certain than the fantasy, because hers was only one side of the tale. Right from the beginning, she and Michael only ever talked of other things, not this. And there had to be collusion before either one of them could risk so much as a stick of the homes they'd built. Her frame held itself constantly open to a bullet or a blow, but she endured because of her faith in a good ending, and because she could convince herself easily enough that where they were then was not where they'd always have to be. But months stretched into a year, then two years, then five. Then uncountable. At some point, her writing softened and stagnated. Somewhere else along that way, other things were lost. Time blurred the edges, fires burned out.

For Thomas, life kept pace with his expectations. All their married life he'd fought hard to keep them in comfort. He paid whenever a bill came due, and worked the long hours without complaint. Caitlin sometimes caught a giveaway hint, a stain or scent, on his shirt collar, but said nothing. Because there was nothing to say. No matter how many times it happened – and it wasn't often but often enough to be considered a relatively regular thing – she'd feel a tuck in her heart. The first few times she'd even cried, but then a feeling of shame would overtake her and she'd drop the shirt into the wash-basket and just walk away, telling herself in such moments that at least he was being discreet, and sensible enough to commit his adulteries on the company's clock.

Things had rusted into place for them as a couple. Silences lasted longer between them, spaces had opened up and they often went entire days without looking one another in the eye. He worked and earned the money, and she, being the one at home, cooked and kept the place clean and tidy, and on evenings when her mood or other exertions put her down or sent her early to bed, the kitchen was always stocked with decent wine and the freezer was always full. He never complained, and most of the time, especially after the first few years, hardly seemed to even notice. Though they stopped short of an outright acknowledgement, they'd become separate people.

One Christmas, the eighth or ninth of their marriage, he gave her a beautiful mid-sized Moleskine notebook with pages a shade of light sepia. Their lives by then were financially comfortable, but gifts never mattered much to either of them. She had the things she needed, and didn't care for the flattery of necklaces and bracelets. The notebook was a token, something to place beneath the Christmas tree alongside the wallet or the tie that she'd wrapped for him.

'Put one of your stories in it,' he'd said, when he picked up on the vagueness of her expression.

She had held the notebook clutched to her chest for several minutes, standing beside the lit tree and gazing out through the window. Snow was falling without hurry on the frozen street, the morning had the twilit heft of chimney smoke, and nothing moved in the world except for the air. In two years she hadn't written so much as a single sentence. That part of who she was had run dry. For a time she'd fought the inevitable, but it was like singing into the wind. She stared into the falling snow and wondered if this was his sweet way of trying to prompt her back into the game, if he'd noticed what was off about her, the firmness gone from her gait, the loss of the tensile strength that had always so gripped her and battened her down when she was in fullest flow. But even as she considered this, she knew it to be false. She doubted that he could remember the last time she'd given him anything of hers, published or otherwise, to read. In his mind, writing was the stuff of hobby, the way all art was, and sport, and anything else that didn't matter one heartbeat to his physical existence, and he indulged her in the same way he'd have indulged her taking up origami or violin lessons or learning to speak Urdu.

His values fit in neat rows. Order matters, or the impression of order, and how you are perceived by the world at large. He is stubborn and single-minded, a sensible, pragmatic, practical man, generous within reason but blind as death to anything set even an inch the wrong side of necessary.

'We might be moving,' he said, one morning ten days or so ago. He'd just drained the last of his coffee and had straightened out the folds in the pages of the newspaper so that it could again appear as new. Part of his routine, the ritual of getting ready to leave for work. 'Illinois.'

She'd just looked at him. The rumour had been in the air a while, though always until now in too flimsy a way to be properly contemplated.

131

'Peoria. Nothing is certain yet, of course. But it could be great for us. It means a big promotion, with a nice bump in salary. And money goes a lot further out there than it does in New York. Peoria's a small city, about three hours from Chicago. We'll buy a house, a nice place. We'll be well set up. The talk is that I stand a good chance, but nothing has been decided yet. I expect to know one way or the other in the next couple of weeks. If it does happen, though, it'll probably come down pretty fast.'

He stood from his place at the table then, and his gaze fell past her to the window beyond, and the dim morning cracking open outside. In his suit, with his chin raised a little, and in the kitchen's raw electric light, he looked handsome, young somehow, a reminder of the man, the boy, she'd married. Spared a glimpse of her own reflection, Caitlin imagined herself at that young age, too, with everything before her, a life yet to be spent. All her mistakes not yet made. The room around them felt as still as a piece of art, with the details as they have always been, and it seemed impossible that the world beneath their feet was turning, and not only turning but spinning wild and hard. He remained in that position for a long moment, frozen into his own past, then nodded his head once, to himself, and left the room, saying his goodbye only when the front door was open in his hand and even then just calling the words back at her, throwing them down behind himself as an afterthought. The door clicked shut before she could raise a response.

If Michael had even once, in all the time they've been together, opened his arms with an offer of catching her, she'd have launched herself out into the abyss for him, happily or in tears but without a single backwards glance. Leaving Thomas seems so much a part of what they both want it clogs the aura of everything that has passed between them and passes still. And yet, it is simplifying the situation to an almost dismissive level. Because the move has never been hers alone to make. By dancing with him that first night, by meeting him again barely twelve hours later for a full-bore follow-up, by sharing everything she had going and everything he had, then and in the decades since, she's already taken herself to the brink. But now, beyond, the great wide open waits.

As a dream, the notion of living together might glitter the way sea will in sunlight, but the reality, she knows, and maybe he knows too, would be thick with a lot more shadow. Yes, they've always longed for more, but not at the risk of sacrificing what's been built. They both understand marriage as a concept and as a practice, with its need for certain pretence and its voids that separate each conceit. As things stand, they have always had the best of both worlds, best in terms of stability and comfort. Nice homes, lives that more or less make sense, a survival fuelled on denial and made bearable by meeting once a month to pleasure in lighting one another's fuses, that four-week integer tried and tested to perfection in their game of lust, gap enough to hone the appetite to aching, to hold excitement at a dizzying height. And even now, after all this time and with the end looming, the possibility of promotion for Thomas and the move to Illinois still just a whisper but growing day by day in clarity and certainty, the sex still has passion, and occasionally, like echo blasts of earlier years, a kind of incandescence, and the talk is sweet, in its small restrictive ways confessional, and as obtusely open as a screaming embrace. What they have going is love. Caitlin has sworn this often to herself, believing it from the inside out, and it makes what they do at least worthwhile if not exactly right. It is love, unquestionably, but love in a rarefied situation, tempered and tuned.

If they only possessed the courage, they'd take hold of one another's hands and jump, damning all consequence. The great wide open awaits, even now, rare with hope and possibility. But the time has already passed for leaps of faith. The world, too fast in spin, has slipped its moorings. Now they are merely hanging on, braced against a different kind of fall.

V

Leave-taking

After the dreams have come, the mornings feel like glass around him. Everything looks too bright, too well preserved. Michael's way of coping is to sit at the kitchen table in silence and try to wait it out. The details of Inishbofin seem layered into the early hour, like an otherworldly second skin, and he fights against closing his eyes so he won't have to acknowledge the faces that hang there, in that darkness, ready to loom, faces that will make him smile to see again but which will also bring deep sadness, because of how they've been lost and long since let go. The house is always still then, silent apart from the acceptable sounds, the clicking of pipes in the walls, water running at a murmur, the paper-weight of his own breath and Barbara's as she idles about small chores, maybe rain against the glass or the crack of snow shifting its weight on the roof. While the coffee percolates, he sits and tries not to move or even think, knowing too well the traps and pitfalls that lie in those directions.

He likes to watch Barbara buttering toast. It's a small thing, but it softens the solitude. She scrapes the slices with a knife, then cuts them into triangles. Her hands have always been delicate, gentle, yet she's good with a knife. And knowing, too, because the angle of the cut seems to matter to the bread's taste. It all goes beyond simple logic. At this stage of their lives, solidly middle-aged, they have dug their rut. On the surface, it's not so bad. In a lit kitchen, Queens can be almost anywhere, and the missing things somehow count for less. The butter is a chemically correct shade of yellow and easily spread, but is actually a type of low-salt-content, sunflower-oil substitute. All along its packaging it boasts in outright lies about the remarkably comparable qualities of its taste. But butter and this stuff only look the same, and appearances will almost always deceive. And, in keeping with this trend, the bread is not real bread either, at least not Michael's definition of real. Finger-thick slices the colour and flavour of dust, with an elasticity that bloats with every chew and which leaves grains of itself on his tongue and in his teeth even after swallowing. Lately, Barb has been pushing for a switch to one of those pro-biotic spreads. The change will make no great difference, since it is all just pseudo-magic anyway, and empty promises, and he'll probably give in, but not yet, because he is stubborn. Healthy diets are all the rage, even among the dying, but he still holds out on a few of the details.

With his attention fixed on such minutiae, entire weeks, months even, can pass without him remembering when the song of the whole world was nothing but the rumble of late-returning boats and the gulls incessant in their screams against the whispering slop of Inishbofin's tide. Or how it felt to stand at his father's side out along the Fawnmore cliffs, knee-deep in the long grass among the scrub of pummelled furze, watching the sun of an August evening melt away as a redness in the west, slathering the ocean first to gold and then to such a damson state that it always seemed like an end to everything instead of merely the closing down of yet another day. The colours of that life remain tucked away inside him, but they exist as a second reality, one that feels better set to dreams.

New York is to blame for this. The girders and stone of the city make such shiftless truth of the here and now, the packed streets, the claustrophobic turmoil of its energy, the soft coaxing of its surfaces belying the hardness of what holds sway beneath. It is as if in accepting one world he cannot quite know the other, because each feels staggered by a distance of galaxies and nothing quite aligns. There are simply too many contradictions to allow a tandem coexistence. And of course, there is the erosion of time to contemplate.

His overwhelming sense, when waking from the old dreams, is generally one of displacement. The air holds all the wrong degrees of lucidity and nothing feels familiar, not the shape of his wife beside but apart from him in the bed or the garbled music weeping in low strains from the clock radio, not the prickling heat of the shower water against his face and body, not the kitchen in which he has sat and greeted decades' worth of dawns. On such occasions, he moves with care, alive to his body's discord, but it is only when he attempts to speak that he truly knows, truly understands. The words that come, the simple utterances towards a good morning, feel awkward and ill-fitting, and older words threaten the surface instead, some of the rasping Irish that goes in grunts and sighs and which he has not spoken in more than half a lifetime, except in small amusement or to indulge an occasional foray into nostalgia, but language as natural to him still as scratching an itch, gentle in story and shaped for knifing through and beneath the winds, shaped for translations of the heart. It is a cracked, ruinous dialect, plush and even amorous in its best moments, at other times scabrous as the flashes and outcroppings of shoreline reef that pock the Atlantic along his birthplace's western front, but a working tongue borne of practicality and bearing little resemblance to the bookish language that they teach in schools nowadays. And evidently, despite the convolutions and splendours of his New York life, it has remained a significant part of who he is.

The problem, one of the many problems, is that the island he holds within himself feels like a lost place. Even upwards of a decade ago, when the telegram arrived announcing the death of Áine, his sister, from something bronchial, a curt three-line note that marked in official terms the severing of his final blood connection to that piece of rock, a good deal of the old life he'd known had already been rendered obsolete, swallowed up by the sweeps of sudden disposable Celtic Tiger wealth that had come pouring out of Dublin and the other boom cities and towns of the Irish mainland during the mid-nineties and the early two thousands.

Time and the grab of money had succeeded in narrowing the span between shores of country and island to something inconsequential, especially during the months outside of winter, and a sea change had occurred. Tourists began to arrive, drawn by the glossy postcard images that represent all the unreality of misty dawns, quaint villages bathed in July hues and the brilliant cinnabar sunsets that burnish the placid Atlantic waters to the west. A trickle, initially, then hordes, backpackers happy with cultivated hardships, wallowing in the squalor of mud and simple fare, the boiled food, the peat fires. Always dressing against the weather and desperate to breathe the lost salt tinge of freedom, to be able to say that they stood a few minutes on a back road, or leaned against the bar in one of the pubs with a pint of stout in hand, chatting through the strains of fiddle music or above the whispers of the nearby tide with those who have lived this way for ever and who have known nothing more nor less of life than this. Spilling off the ferries in groups and families, from everywhere but mainly from Britain or the States, people who've made their choice to break this year from burned beaches and the centres of defined culture – Paris, Rome, Barcelona, Vienna, even Dublin – and to hunt instead for the authentic, the special something that they feel has been too long missing from their particular take on the world.

So Inishbofin flourishes, even as it loses something of itself. Progress, they call that, the ones who keep office hours in big cities and who need a word to justify the small devastations they inflict on time. Tourists bring money, and everyone needs that, because bartering has long since fallen out of fashion, and because the fish lessen in number with every passing year.

But that's not the place he knows, and that knows him. To close his eyes is to return to an older world, and it's all there, layers of it, soft memories coated in hard shells, pained moments that even now, after so long, have lost nothing of their ache.

It's natural, of course, to reminisce, especially as a heart settles into middle age, and regret is a flavour familiar to anyone who has ever fled one life in the chase for another. Michael was sixteen when he left, and mired in some half-formed state between childhood and the ways of adults. Most of the time, he clings to this as his excuse. And, most of the time, it is enough. But the truth is that he'd already felt the loom of an end.

Some weeks prior to his going, they'd been down in the bottom field, laying out a turf rick, and the old man had straightened from a stoop, tossed down an armful of clods and gone to lean against the wall. His mouth hung open and his staring eyes shone dark against the waxy flats of his face. Weariness was part of it, but levels of exhaustion were facts of their lives and this was something more convoluted, something vampiric.

'We'll stop a while, boy,' he said, once he felt certain of his breath. 'Sure, there's legs in the day yet.'

Michael stared, then averted his gaze, electing to consider instead the rash of cloud that cloaked without quite obliterating the colourless smudge of sun, and, when that didn't feel like enough, the rough-cut chunks of turf which lay scattered around his boots. He felt a longing to sit, too, and the support of the stone wall looked inviting, but he allowed himself only a minute's pause before bending again to the chore, knowing that the day would not end for them until the work did. He gathered up the bricks of turf, stacked them as he'd been shown so many times, laying them into place thick-side down, sod-side up so that the rick could waterproof itself over months' worth of drying time. Working steadily and without much thought, focusing on nothing but the order of the job, focusing least of all on the ache that had sunk as a chill into the low of his back. Cold grey mud packed the folds of his neck and coated his hands like a leprous second skin, and he tasted and breathed it, feeling the sourness of its soupy grit between his back teeth whenever he clenched his jaw. There was no way to erase what he'd glimpsed, but island boys and men know well enough what fits the silence and what does not, and the shadow that greyed and blunted Seán seemed a harbinger, of sorts. His father did not die that day in the field, or even that year, but he did seem to skirt a brow of some hill around that time, because what followed was degrees of slow, meticulous disintegration.

That day, stacking the turf, Michael considered the old man's blanched expression, the accepted horror within the downturned eyes, the mouth that sucked and bubbled like a stab wound, rabid for the cold refreshing air, and the image that stormed his mind was of his mother laid out in a lamplit bedroom, dead at barely thirty and looking as if she had never lived at all. An aneurysm of some sort, a sudden thunder crack that ripped her from the world and reduced her to that smoke-yellowed mannequin state, mute as space and stiffer than any bone, her raven hair unnaturally flat without the pull of wind to turn it feral, tendrils of fringe boxing in her broad forehead. Because he'd been so young, the details of that earlier time seem detached from one another and have to be stitched together with lines of logic. But he does remember that, after the sun went down, the house had quickly filled, and through most of the night people continued to arrive, women from all over the island carrying cakes or plates of cold sliced meat, men laden with dark unmarked bottles and jugs of stout or hauling sacks of pigs' trotters that would be left to simmer for hours and soften to a state of almost unbelievable sweetness.

Initially, he'd had a place to sit, a piece of couch cushion that he was forced to share with Áine but which still afforded comfort. Then, as the space thinned, he was moved and resettled on the flagstones beside the empty fire and given no choice but to stand. Áine kept him at her side and held his hand, with their fingers tightly entwined. Her intent was to discourage thoughts of escape, but it was an unnecessary precaution. Fear kept him still, fear that was different from the anxiety he felt for strange soundings in the night or those things the darkness masked. Because this time the worst had already happened, and the aftermath lay before him as a hole in the world, gaping and immutable.

His mind that night of his mother's wake was full of many things, but heaviest in his thoughts was a memory of something she had once said, months or a year earlier, her voice exasperated and yet full of compassion as she knelt before him to wrap a piece of cotton gauze around yet another of his badly skinned knees: 'You know, Michael,' she'd said, 'if you don't run so much, you won't fall so much.' Standing holding hands with Áine in that crowded living room, he let those words roll through his mind, and there was still a sense of calm to be had from the gentle remembered float of her voice. But from the little he'd glimpsed through the bedroom door, the previous night and again that morning, stillness seemed to him a far worse fate than falling. Surely there were times when the feel of all that chasing energy was more than worth the tumble, and the skinned knee. He didn't fully understand what had happened but sensed enough to realise what death must mean, and it was the reverence that the word earned which made him feel so afraid. Beside him, Áine's breathing had the thin, put-upon texture of shocked calm, and her fingers between his were cold and dry, as if some essence of who she was had retreated, taking all her heat with it. But he was glad of the touch, glad of the promised reassurance offered by skin against his skin. They stood there, breathing the good wintry aroma of the sweet-boiling trotters thickening the air and insinuating every pore, afraid to speak but watching the tide of faces that they knew well, neighbours bunched in groups, their cheeks reddened from whiskey, their mood sombre, especially as the light softened and was lost and the time came for lanterns to be lit. Each was sincere in his or her grief, but it was different for them, a passing thing. They were saddened that one of their own had been lost to them, but the equilibrium of their world at least held its level.

Across the room, ignored by everyone, Seán sat on the edge of a hard chair, head bowed, weeping. A strapping man, softened. Sometimes, when the packed bodies parted just enough, Michael could see his big shoulders heaving against the punch of tears, and whenever the murmured conversations hit a lull, the sound of his pain carried throughout the house, forlorn as the lowing of something bestial across a span of valleys and fields. That weeping continued for hours, and through the terrible days that followed. It shook him and shook them all as they huddled together at the heart side of the sloping graveyard's opened ground while rain lashed their faces, and it continued after they had returned home and were swallowed up once more into that small house's dense gloom. But at some point it did soften and eventually it stopped altogether, to be replaced with the kind of silence that told its own story.

Glimpsed through a doorway left ajar, death for Michael is and will always be a curtained bedroom yellowed and set off-kilter by a burning lantern, and on the bed a face too still, known but no longer quite right, the muscles too relaxed, the shape pulled slack in every wrong direction. Calm, but too still. Once seen, it had felt a thing impossible to forget, or deny, yet somehow and for a long time he managed to succeed in doing both. But that day with his father in the field, the month or so before his leaving, there it was again. Not the same, but with enough similarity to make him remember. He stacked the turf, watched the old man with snatched glances, and thought of how things would be a year from now. And he began to think about running.

People die every day; the world is full of little voids. His mother had slipped from a living, breathing, laughing state to a still and yellowy husk, and part of the overgrown hillside, tucked beneath the winds and crooked stones. And not alone either, but there with her people, the old stock who lived and died before Michael's time as well as the minutes' worth of unnamed younger sister that he'd seen only as a dreamy blueness through a grey, threadbare bed sheet and in his mind, in the darkness, can sometimes see still. That hillside bulged, with his mother and the rest, but still the shadow roamed, insatiable, seeking and marking out, separating weaklings for the cull.

In a city like New York, in a city like Dublin, even, no one thinks this way, not like they can and frequently do in country places and on islands. In the cities, steel and stone are the tangibles, and death is just death, a fact of life and an end to things. No hoods, no scythes, no shadows, no capital letters. In the cities, stories are for the pages of books. Told sometimes to pleasure or to scare, but not believed, at least not to a level where belief gets to dictate. Neither ides nor omens for New York, London, Paris, Dublin, only facts. It has to do with different sets of freedoms.

On those mornings after the dreams have come, Barbara brings coffee and sits with her back to the windows, facing the open kitchen door so that she can see through into the hallway. Always waiting for something, some news from afar, even if it's just the morning paper. Sometimes she hums little snatches of whatever song she has woken with in her mind. And when the stillness becomes too much, she rises again, and switches on the radio. It is always the same, a grumbling of static, music jerking in and out of tune, and then either a news station or something gentle and innocuous, sixties and seventies hits, but with the volume kept low. They listen, finish their coffee and toast, then reach for bowls and the cereal. These days, they eat muesli. Eggs are high in cholesterol, and bacon has become like a swear word, but muesli is meant to be good for the heart, or the bowels, or something.

The whole thing is a farce, shadow play. After the dreams have come and the bounds of time have been broken, what is gone feels far more immediate, more enlivened, than what tries to count as the here and now. And such mornings fill Michael with the sensation of having been cast adrift. He sips the coffee and quietly digests his breakfast, knowing that he properly belongs nowhere. As good as New York has been to him, he'll never understand the city on a conspiratorial level. Because he was not born for these streets. Barbara, who is full of her own concerns, seems content in leaving him to his silence, but he knows that, were she to press for conversation, his words would come only and ever in Irish. This would probably amuse and then frighten her, and the thought of it frightens him too, because he senses that once he started there'd be no stopping, that it would be like splitting an artery. He chews the muesli and keeps his eyes open, inhaling with care because the bare stone walls of his father's cottage feel suddenly only a breath away, the small kitchen window coated with the salt and grit of the sea wind and whistling draughts where the sealing putty has crusted and turned to powder. If he tries at all, he can feel the heavy wool of an old sweater across his back and shoulders, a thing passed down, the thick shape of it sagging around him several sizes too big, but its weight comforting against the bleak days, its odour filling his mouth with sooty, slightly gamey sweetness, a familiar taste that itches his tongue and lights a fire deep

146

down in his throat. And when the wind catches just right in the eaves, it can pass, almost, for the high keening of Áine, deep in one of the ancient laments she so loved to sing, and it takes nothing at all to imagine her busying herself with collecting breakfast eggs from the small coop or struggling with a slopping pail of water from the communal pump at the bottom of the hill.

Inishbofin is home, even still, but the connections to the place are too long lost, the damage irreparable. Seán dead and buried within a few years of Michael's leaving, Áine also gone. There were the boys, her sons, his nephews, three of them, steps of stairs, but they are grown men now and have themselves long since abandoned the island. They have his address but none of them have kept in touch, as so often happens. They can't be blamed. They don't know him. He's a name, that's all, a nowhere man and a nobody. Someone they will have heard their mother mention, someone to look up if they ever happen to find themselves in New York, who can speak, if pressed, as they do and who will offer food and a bed, money, if needs be. He is nothing to their lives, but even though he only knows them from the flattened expressions of the photographs that Áine used to send every Christmas time without fail, they are, in a way, everything to him. Because they remain the last surviving links to his past, to who he was before he started trying so hard to be someone else.

Caitlin loves listening to him speak of the island. He always feels an initial reluctance, even though the thoughts remain a constant part of who he is. But she knows what to say, and how to open him up. She has an image of Ireland already in her mind from the pictures she has seen and from her mother's occasional stories, but Michael can give her stone and dirt, a sense of that world outside of poetry, musing about how he'd like to go back, some day, just to see the place again. Just to reconnect with all that he has lost and left behind. His craving to return is tempered by the knowledge that Inishbofin holds nothing for him any more, nothing beyond the simply nostalgic, but there is comfort to be had from wishing. And halving his memories with someone who actually wants to hear, who wants to be able to taste and feel what he already knows, makes all the difference. On some level, they both understand that this is nothing more than talk, of the sort that lovers often share in an effort to compensate for all that must remain missing between them, and to play up to the delusion that what they have together is something more substantial than the facts might otherwise suggest. But for her, most of the time, it is enough, because his voice becomes imbued with a melancholy that allows for another and particular kind of intimacy, a deep uncovering of who he is or once was. It's a sharing of dreams, and when the subject breaks the surface, she nestles against him in bed, inclines her head so that her forehead can feel the brush of his unshaven cheeks, and prompts him with little sounds from the low part of her throat, urging him on.

He remembers a day when they had even spoken of going together. Fantasy, of course, and impossible from the first suggested word, but a nice idea to play with for a while. That day feels close, too, the way so much of the past does, another bitter winter's afternoon somewhere in the height of summer, years gone now yet still alive somehow, still delicious in its details. They've known a lot of such afternoons together, and this one – whenever it was – is another of those that have become tangled in some universal cog and now plays out endlessly, just beneath the skin of usual daily living. Reach out in the right direction and it's there, just one of the hundreds, a sigh or a gasp away.

With the least effort, he can feel again the lunchtime hour, and the hard-starched linen sheets of yet another strange bed as they came together, filling one another's arms in the aftermath moments of what they'd really come here to do, but holding her body tightly to his own so that their feet lay tangled and their hips and shoulders touched, and describing in drowsy whispers the winters that shaped his childhood. Everything else changes but seasons only shift, and winters now can only ever know the colours and weight of all those that have gone before. Days when the wind hit gale force and waves lashed the western shore with enough violence to send the roars of war clear across the island, and there was nothing left to do except get inside and either perch by the window to watch the sweeps of rain blotting the landscape or else pull a chair in close to the fire and try to find comfort in how the small heroic colours of the flames raged in combat against the chimney's gloom. Winter kept the boats anchored off the pier, those that had a choice in the matter, and brought the sort of weather that turned the hours ripe for stories and recollections.

Tourism has undoubtedly shifted the island's inner equilibrium, but because of his early desertion the Inishbofin of his childhood remains preserved, with the home-place winters enduring most vividly, and it is these that he finds himself missing most of all. Because as good as summers are to little boys so full of running, and as beautiful, wild and tormented, Inishbofin at that time of year always had less about it, somehow, less to mark it out as distinct from the rest of the world. At least on a scale of any magnitude. The summers were days of glory, the mornings spent out along the beaches, paddling up to his knees in the cold blue foamy water, leaving his clothes on to swim or else stripping completely naked so that he could feel the sun all over his body and the grubby cling of the salt and the wet sand against his skin. Or flinging ancient serpentine hand grenades overarm out into the tide in defence against imagined invaders, or playing hiding games of Pirate in the shallow inlet caves. When his heart had pounded its fill, gathering whelks and cockles from among the rocks for Áine to boil in peppery milk and to serve as lunch with soda bread still warm from the early bake. And when enough heat had infiltrated the day and the salted air began to crackle, using the hours until evening either catching frogs or plundering nests, settling mostly for the cream and speckled sandpiper eggs laid down like bowled stones in the grassy verges of the higher ground out along Knock Head, but living really for the lucky days of certain shine, when everything fell right and he'd chance searching for the corncrake's greenish-grey fool's gold treasury hidden and waiting waist-deep in the hay fields with harvest-time drawing near. Those were the clotted facts of the high season and the rhythms of a slamming heart, but if they live on as perfect days in memory then they are also too pure, too distilled. And in the same way that hurt lingers as long or longer than laughter, it is the more visceral winter memories, all raw edges, that continue to captivate his senses. The hard stones of rain in his face, the cold smoking magic, the cleave of the wind and the constant savagery of the ground beneath his feet. Summers were for smiling, but winters held the attention of more serious considerations. Winters, with their heavy seas and their evening murk always whitening and smothering the daylight hours, drew in the edges of the world and made the existence of the old gods seem possible again.

He understands that, if he were to go back now, or five or ten years from now, the winters probably would retain at least some of their gloriously cruel physical aspects, the gales still chasing in hard to lash the shoreline and the fields, the roads still masked in bitter mist and silent as stone of passers-by, and the men who fish still giving their attentions to the piling of the storm cloud before venturing out anyway, knowing too few alternatives. But despite the unchanging details, something would be different, at a physical or psychological level, because the island has opened up, and circumstances have suffered the beneficial traumas of influx and money, new people, new ideas, new ways of life. Inishbofin will have found a new reality, one in which he'd no longer quite fit.

The idea of them making a shared trip has always been a thing to say, part of the game.

'So, it's settled then?' Caitlin said, that winter's afternoon back in, what – the early nineties? As if it were simply a matter of deciding.

He remembers laughing. 'What will Thomas say? Or Barbara?'

But she'd only pressed him with her smile.

'Don't worry about them. I'll come up with a story, concoct a great-aunt or something. I'm a writer. I'm paid to deceive.'

'Of course. Sorry.'

'At least, I was, for about five minutes, once upon a time. But I'd back myself to still be able, when needs must. And you're easy. Travel is part of your programme anyway. So, a selling trip. Chicago, say. Or Seattle. A whistle-stop tour. Five, six towns in as many nights. And just think of it. We'd have a whole week to ourselves. Just like real people. Like a real couple. And you can give me the guided tour, even though I feel like I know the place already, from all the years of listening to you talk. And because I know you.'

'You have it all figured out.'

'Just say you'll think about it. Please, Mike.'

'I'm thinking about it now,' he told her, smirking so that the words took on a wider meaning, and she coughed a little laughter even through his closing kiss.

Only in the intimacy of an illicit bed could there have been any chance, however slim, of their going. In a bed rented by the hour and where and when everything said, done and thought was a thoroughgoing lie anyway, or at least a fantasy. The tip of her tongue trawled the crater of his upper lip, and he realised yet again that he'd never known such a magnitude of sharing, both bodily and of the soul, with anyone else.

His throat felt thick with an old thought, but it caught on a heavy sigh and was smashed to pieces of its worth. *Tá grá agam duit*; words that he had never before spoken, not to anyone, not even to those who'd have been in desperate need of hearing them said. *I love you.* That afternoon, though, he closed his eyes and spoke, whispered, and the sentiment, without translation, hung almost shape-less between them, flushed by air of its edges, and so much the better for that. Caitlin stretched her body into his and smiled, at him and at something deep inside herself, and misreading his words as mere sound, let them slip away.

That last night before his leaving, a gulf already lay vast and empty between father and son, fathoms of silence pinning them down while the turf in the fireplace burned shades of fox-fur and rose hip. The old man was probably mid-fifties then, certainly no more than that, an age not terribly much in numbers but one which lay heavy on frame and face. The firelight brightened surfaces, and the lines that creased his brow and cheeks seemed cut with such severe definition that every shift for breath and considered thought announced itself anew. His eyes held the void and looked big and heavy in their trance, and his hair, usually the colour of week-old snow, had become again the muddy, summer-night red of better times.

Fifty here could be old, with the days and nights mounted hard, one upon the next. In the fields or out on the water through the heavy months, with the westerly ocean wind lacing fatigue into backs and shoulders and with the low seething skies that brought rain clouds in rafts set so barely apart that all the world but rock was breaths of green, even the best of men were broken into compliance. Like most of the islanders, Seán lived for the dark, loamy earth and, on the off-days, the ocean. Working a small boat that he and his brother, Tadhg, had inherited from their father, timing the shoals, keeping to the areas of water known without need of charts, harvesting the mackerel when they came and the herring that had been so plentiful before the Spanish and Scandinavian trawlers took to working the international line. Tadhg, six years the senior, had been overboard twice in storms and sometimes wept when it rained. His second time over had seen him nine hours in the water and presumed lost, and the salt had so corroded his vocal cords that speaking hurt him for years afterwards. In the boat, he kept a three-foot slab of driftwood always within easy reach, preferring that to a life jacket, trusting the natural buoyancy of the wood over anything man-made. Survival for Seán and Tadhg and their kind was earned by days on the water and longer ones, slavish hours in every weather, bound to a piece of land, a few rock-strewn acres that offered frugal security but demanded devotion. Seán gave the years of his life to one and the other, and he met the nights, especially after his wife's passing, famished for a plate of whatever Áine served up, fish or mutton stew, and afterwards a glass or two of something that would settle him with his thoughts beside the fire, whiskey on special occasions, more usually porter or the illegal sheer-proof poitín that found its way up out of the island's hidden places, distilled from potatoes and barley and concealed in old unmarked milk bottles. 'A taste,' he'd say, to hide any embarrassment, having accidentally broken into song, 'just to keep the badness out.' And he'd smile then at Áine or at Michael with all the melancholy in his heart and explain that there was nothing like the poitín for warding off colds, and sometimes he'd draw them near and let them indulge in a little sip, just so that he could pleasure in their exaggerated reactions. But he was always careful to heed his own limit, the second glass, except if they happened to be entertaining a visitor or if it was some better juice on the go, at Christmas time, New Year's, or some such night worthy of the marking.

At the fireside, Michael drained his second glass and felt the life of the whiskey on his tongue and then a sense of loss as its heat began to fade. His father reached again for the bottle.

'Not for me, Dad. I've an early start in the morning.'

'You can have one more, boy. Sure you'll be gone long enough. Hold up your glass.'

He hesitated, then lifted his glass towards the waiting bottle. The whiskey had done something, had slackened him, and the chair now wanted all his weight. He felt the weariness hanging from his body like a soaked coat. He waited through the pouring, then sat back and, just for a second, closed his eyes.

When he met the room again, new life had come into the fire, gouts of yellow that burned like a bright heart inside the night. Twenty years later, lying naked in that anonymous hotel bed and recalling for the first time with anyone those moments of leave-taking, he'll open his eyes to the exact inverse of this sensation, to a room bleeding out of its afternoon light, the whiteness greying and growing mute. Even as the days themselves fade like footsteps in sand, memories hold frozen. And even as the light begins to die, he'll reach out for Caitlin, desperate to catch the details before they shift. He'll notice everything then:

155

the moist gleam that her tongue leaves across her lower lip; her thin forearms veiled in a down fine and shining as hoarfrost; the somehow cool inner surface of her right thigh when he traces it with his mouth from above her knee and which echoes heartbeat when he presses his ear hard to it and dares listen. Against him, she'll writhe as indolently snakelike as a thread of extinguished candle smoke, and they'll smile and talk in murmurs and fall each in turn upon the other, and the world will be soundless apart from the noises they make, their voices twinned in hushed promise, the static charge of their breathing, and the joints of the bed beneath them in full, relentless moan. So many worlds, each its own reality, exist within breaths, and all it takes to pass between them is to close off one and open onto another. Motes of life get trapped, something gets noticed in a way that can never be undone, a widening of eyes, hair spilling in certain fashion darkly over skin or across the snow-white pillow, an unexpected stiffening or collapse of light. And the moment is caught, like in a photograph only more fully blown, with all its senses intact.

He studied the fire. As a child the flames had captivated him, lapping at the turf and dancing in fringes along the thin bark of the hedge kindling. That fire had become his vision of Hell, some mindset encouraged by what the missionary priests talked about whenever they landed on the island and took over the church. Hell as a scalding redness, not yet understanding how far that was from the truth.

'I'm going,' he muttered. 'My mind is made up. You can't talk me out of it.'

The words met at first with silence and were left to fall away, and he felt relief but also a twinge of hurt at the idea that he'd somehow read the situation wrong. He wanted his going to be easy, on everyone. But not too easy. And the exhaustion he felt only deepened his confusion.

'If I can't, I can't,' his father replied, after allowing several seconds to pass. 'I know the story well enough. It's the way of the young to want to run.' His eyes considered the glass, held up like something precious on a perch of ravaged fingertips, and his mouth shifted in search of more to say, the right words. But instead of speaking, he went into the whiskey, his stubble-ridden chin jogging with the effort. At that moment, backed as he was in shadow, he looked not just old but ancient. And nearly broken.

They drank together; Michael, even relatively new to whiskey as he was, following the lead, feeling this as a prelude to the end. The fire was there still but burning down, and three glasses had to be the limit. But then the old man cleared his throat.

'I never told you, or Áine either, but when I was a boy, just about the age you are now, I wanted to go to London. Word had it that there was plenty of work going and heaps of money to be made, and it took all we could do back then just to put a few spuds or a bite of bread on the table. I was great with one of the Shine lads from Cloonamore. Dan Joe, God be good to him.'

'He'd be Sonny Shine's uncle.'

'That's right. Ned, his brother, is Sonny's father. Ned was that bit younger, but me and Dan Joe were the one age. I suppose we grew up together. And he was always

157

on about London. Never shut up about the place. Though the truth of it, looking back, is that I was probably just as bad.'

He sipped again from his glass, rationing it now, knowing that the night's quota had been reached, knowing too that this should not have mattered but, for some unaccountable reason, did. 'Stupid,' he whispered, so low that Michael leaned in, sure that he'd misheard.

'What happened?'

'Nothing. I discovered that I was suited to home. And whether you realise it or not, boy, so are you.' He turned then and met Michael's stare, and his mouth fractured with an uncertain grin. 'Don't worry, I'm not trying to persuade you. I waste enough of my breath as it is. You have your own mind, and you'll make it up as you see fit. Christ, I can't account for all this talk. It must be the whiskey. A good drop can do that to a man. And you should see what it can do to a woman. Well, you will see, I suppose, in time to come. Everyone sees everything eventually, I think. The things that matter, anyway. But I suppose I wanted to tell you something about myself, something you didn't already know and that you could take with you when you leave here. Because I might not get the chance again.'

The words, said in so casual a manner, made the moment seem part of the everyday, the every-night, and not at all the turning of new ground. A father and his only son pushed so closely together by circumstance, they'd grown accustomed to and tolerant of one another's ways. But even though they lived and ate together and spent the bulk hours of each day working side by side in the fields or on the boat, they rarely spoke beyond surfaces.

Growing up, Michael had been full of questions, though he was never aimless in his asking. By ten or twelve, he'd developed a thoughtful, even ponderous nature, of a sort that might still have yearned for wildness but which also needed fixed limits, edges to the world's pictures. He wanted to get at the reasons for things, to catch a glimpse of the mechanics beneath the casing. How the fields knew when to flower, why the fish came at certain times of year and why always to the same waters when there were all the oceans of the world in which to swim. What life had been like back in his grandfather's day, or his great-grandfather's, during the times of hunger and the British. And why some people had more than others, and what made anyone want to live on an island when everything was so easily to hand in the big cities, everything but open skies. The answers, such as they were, leaned uncertain against the walls of day, Seán speaking without even straightening from whatever task lay at hand, his voice thick as storm-water sluicing in the grassy roadside gullies, drunk-sounding, on the edge of song, speaking some lament led only by its grief. Unfurling names, places and stories overlooked by history books but which had proven too significant for oblivion. And alongside, Michael kept on, even at eight, ten, twelve years old, letting his hands in mimicry rebind the nets where the reefs had split them open, or swinging the borrowed second scythe in low left-to-right sweeps, canting his way through the shins of hay or barley. And though in physical terms he focused strictly on his work, his mind was tuned fast to the things his father said, and he listened with fullest concentration, absorbing the words, the voice, the educating facts. He

159

knew that the world had existed for ever, especially out here, where the air hung thick as mist with legend, the white cow tales that named the island and the sagas of Gráinne Ní Mháille, *Granuaile*, the Pirate Queen. But even with the stony evidence of Dún Mór, the Westquarter's ancient ruined promontory fort, stacked high for him, even with the scars of Cromwell still tattooed into the ether and the crumbling or levelled famine shells mottling the fields along the many boreens, such past still felt theoretical rather than real, in the same way as the godly distances between stars or the notion that fire, earth and water live and breathe. These things mattered, but for him, at that age, darker and more intimate curiosities lay boxed within the silences, to do with his own blood. His mother had been a Flaherty, and centuries-sprung from this rock, a clan renowned on Bofin and, once upon a time, on neighbouring Shark. He longed but only occasionally dared to raise her as the subject, wanting to know who she had been but cautious of the heartache that he might awaken, recollecting too vividly the blacked-out months of grief which had followed her passing. When he did ask, after gauging the old man's mood as good or at least approachable, he kept to the inanities that brought her to mind for them both while at the same time holding her at a safe distance. What she'd been like, beyond the stiffness of their few photographs and the crumbling memories that seemed less real with every passing year. Because even back then, the details of who she was had largely slipped from his grasp. There were nights still when he dreamed of her, and he knew her face without being able to quite focus on it, but the sense of her touch

160

was becoming lost to him. Her voice, too. He couldn't have sworn to the colour of her eyes or the make-up of her laughter. Even her smile was drifting beyond his reach into half-imagined shapes. And his father's voice in answering always came carefully, as if speaking of a stranger, or of someone he knew but did not know well. She was of people made and meant for this place, Seán said, and for the ocean. The men, her father, her father's brothers, knew the water better than anyone anywhere, they could have closed their eyes for a month and still circled the island clockwise and back, marking every current. They were hard, good people, honest in their dealings, but she herself, Bríd, was something else entirely, something infinitely more. 'My wife,' he'd add, as if needing the proof of such confirmation, and as if stating it could make it that much more real. 'Your mother. Yours and Áine's.' A woman possessed of a sweet, wholesome nature, gentle as dew, without a strain of anger or unease in her body or mind. Beautiful, if you had it in you to look in just such a way. All she knew was love, and how to love, and she'd been taken far too soon, the way the best ones often are. That had angered him for the longest time, until he accepted that life keeps its own rules, and until he learned to sustain himself on memories of the years she'd been able to give. The heavy words caught their cadence and rattled tightly to one another, the way bees drone inside the hive, all echo, their noise far too big and boisterous for their shape, but lulling. His eyes remained downcast and the work continued, hands threshing, or pulling stones, or hauling in the nets, back bent in gravitational press against the sloping of the land

161

or braced to ride the rolls of ocean, but his talk fell in gluts, like syrup from a spoon, slowly torrential, unwinding memories of how she had been on any of a thousand nights spent welcoming his return, her dark hair maddened by the field winds, her weather-baked skin looking yellow-white as buttermilk through the clotted kitchen dusk. Those were the happy times, the painted moments, said Seán, addressing only the dirt, thinking aloud, yet even in the throes of this confession there was the sense of something being held back. And Michael, doing only what he could, grasped the fragments and read life into them, grateful even for that much. They were used to half-talk, conversations bulked out with nods and shrugs, their stoicism generations imbued. Silence was the strength of men and boys. Troubles of a more intimate nature were brought to Áine, who never laughed at anything, never teased or condemned, only tightened her jaw and dealt with what she could. This was the way of things.

At the fireside, that last night, cradling the glass in both hands, the temptation for Michael was to offer some argument, for his father's sake and for his own, some insistence that of course they'd see one another again, that there were years left to them yet, more than time enough for everything to be said and done. But every sip of whiskey further repressed the words and, for something to do, he took up the iron poker and stirred the embers. The fire, which had stilled to a soothing blend of warmth and colour, erupted in small explosions, a clod of turf shifted and then split apart, opening craters like gasping inhalations before collapsing inward in jags of flame and avalanches of ash. Seán leaned forward too, as though

162

overseeing the operation, clutching his own glass but not drinking, and Michael knew the old man was holding back the little that remained because he liked to take the taste of the whiskey to bed with him.

'Everyone at home told me not to go. My mother said the English had enough of their own and that they wouldn't thank me for intruding. Of course, I thought different. At that age, I knew everything there was to know.'

Understanding came slowly. Michael, somewhat distracted, focused on the idea of his old man not old at all but a teenager and with everything in terms of living still to come. He set the poker down.

'You mean to say that you actually went?'

'I did.'

'Jesus.'

'Michael.'

'Sorry, Dad. But why didn't you say so before now?'

'I don't know why. I suppose it no longer seemed to matter. What's done is done, and it was all such a long time ago. Until recently, I'd more or less stopped thinking about it.'

Now it was Michael who reached for the bottle. It sat on the floor beside his father's chair, and felt cold to his touch. He splashed a tot into his own glass, then waited at a tilt until the old man finished the little that he'd been holding back.

'So? How was it?'

His father thought about it, and shrugged. 'Home was better.'

Then, having committed to revealing something precious of himself, he seemed to retreat again, and he sipped from his glass, indulging his natural introversion. Michael waited without pressing, feeling an unexpected contentment. Exhaustion played a part, as did the alcohol, but even in the darkness some filament of clarity had offered itself. Sharing sixteen years of days spent working from hand to hand and nights tucked beneath the thatch, confined to a few cramped rooms and eating food hard-boiled and over-fried, drinking mugs of tea so hot from the pot crooked over the fire and stewed to such strength that it hurt your throat to swallow, talking but only ever of menial things, knowing well the ways of one another, knowing best of all the sounds of one another's breath. But that night, it was whiskey, and the certain sense that they had never been as close as this.

Home was better. Over another hour of clumsy, whiskey-fuelled meandering, Michael's father felt his way towards explanation by describing deplorable working and living conditions, the nights wasted in stupor, the men, sometimes even workmates, friends of sorts, found beaten unconscious in alleyways behind late bars or strip clubs and, on one occasion, even stabbed to death, murdered for having offended with the wrong accent or for the couple of pounds of pay, the few remaining coins balled into a small note, in a coat pocket. But such rambling talk distilled easily down to this one irrefutable essence: home was better. And in that hotel room all the years later, listening to it told afresh and repeating the words to herself in a kind of hum, Caitlin sat up from the pillow of Michael's chest and perched for some time, seconds or minutes, on the edge of the bed, gazing out of the window with her back turned to him. Her naked skin, where it showed through from beneath the raven tendrils of her loosened hair, shone a different shade of white from the whiteness of the afternoon, pale but spoiling towards the faintest tan.

'And was it better?' she asked, without turning, trusting enough in the tone of his reply, and perhaps also wanting to let them each feel this beat of separation.

'I suppose so,' Michael said, and reached out to stroke her cooling flesh, tracing the venetian lattice of her ribs where they bent inside the press of her right elbow and her upper arm. 'For him, anyway.'

He smiled at his answer, not understanding quite why but helpless against the rise of it, and she turned her face in profile, just for a second, and seeing all there was to see, couldn't help but smile, too, maybe wanting to share in whatever was really happening, whatever was actually being said. Then she returned her gaze to the glass, and to the piece of Coney Island sky that stretched beyond, a matted screed of cloud empty of detail, at that moment a sky like any other sky.

'He meant it as a warning, of course,' she added, just before getting up to dress.

'Of course.' Michael, possibly attuned to the imminence of their parting, and resisting, let his hand climb nearly to the nape of her neck before scrying slowly downwards, and his mouth remembered the taste of that skin from less than an hour earlier, when he had rolled her over onto her stomach and kissed the full length of her spine up into the loose nest of her hair and ever so slowly back again, delighting all the while in how she'd trembled and called out in shy anticipation, asking him onwards.

'And he meant well. The old man always meant well, in everything he said and did. But he was talking about a long time ago, when the world was a different place.'

Caitlin listened, then turned and held his hand. At this point in time, his body had yet to bloat, and she considered him, taking in the bareness of his chest with its nipples ringed in webs of dark and already silvering hair, and then his throat and the first hint of softness beneath his chin, and finally, almost in afterthought, the details of his face. He lay back and waited, as he'd grown accustomed to doing, for her gaze to rise, and grinned in welcome, but she did not smile back and her trance never wavered. Even when their eyes met, he found her somehow out of focus with the surface. Her hand remained in his, slight and fragile and notably cold, but she kept to her pose. He watched the fingers of her free hand explore the inside of his wrist, her nails, trimmed but not too short and painted just for him in the deep terracotta shade of roof tiles and first blood, seeming like the only gesture towards colour in the whole room. Nothing could be hidden, naked in the moment as they found themselves, and yet so much stood between them, the things known and the things denied.

There was always more to say, on both sides, but words made the leaving terribly hard. Finally, still entranced, still dreaming, she had slipped from the bed and begun to dress. Something within the colourless construct of the room should have changed, a shifting of the world felt overdue. Yet all was stillness. He watched her drag her black lace panties up her thighs, and everything about her boasted the subtle grace of someone trained to the

166

stage, bending the way swans will in seeking the sun. And soundless, having stepped away from him, having already committed to going. Buttoning her blouse, pulling on her sweater, fixing her hair. Month after month it was the same, variations on the by-then familiar tune. His leaving home had played out in nothing like such calm. Full with the need to go, and telling himself as much, over and over, so that he wouldn't hesitate, yet doing so just the same, lingering. As he stood in the doorway with the cottage to his back, dawn had broken across the fields, undoing the stitches of darkness, and the sky was a sheet of cloud, resembling from behind glass how the sky looked on any particular lost-and-found winter's day out over Coney Island. At sixteen he was already broad across the chest, not yet a man but neither any longer a child, given to stillness from time spent on the water and squatting in field corners, understanding of the balance in all things, innocent enough still to believe in dreams and beating like a drum to run, but not yet set for such a wrenching. The air was cool and salted from the sea, and pure in a way that it would never quite seem for him again, except by suggestion, except on the very occasional spring or a late September day when another ocean or another side of this one happened to hold a swell and the wind blew just right. Behind him, in the dark of the cottage, his father sat at the kitchen table, head bowed over a mug of hot tea, while across the room, in the chair beside the burned-out fire, Áine wept, her fist clenching and relaxing around an old handkerchief that she held pressed to her lips in an effort to quell the tiny rumblings of her sobs. She was already married by then, and pregnant to a point just

167

beginning to show; barely twenty but bulked and rubbed to a state of middle age. Her hands had the alabaster shine of cold-water work, and her hair, the bronzed red of teak and wild as bracken, spilt heavy around her shoulders. Tears came, in a strained, wrenching way familiar to their kind, and she let them fall. And caught between turning back and wanting to get away, Michael held himself in that doorway as the darkness broke and over the following minutes turned pale and then colourless, and he gazed out across the fields and the water beyond, trying to draw the flavours of the island inside himself, trying to gather in the small noises of the dawn, the birds in song, the thrushes and finches in the hedgerows, stonechats and pipits, the jerking pulse of a far-off cuckoo, and down by the shore-line the punctuating screams of the fulmars or the gulls as they circled to trail the leaving boats. Then, finally, his attention was snagged by a more sudden sound, that of the old man pushing his chair backwards on the flagstone floor and getting up to move around the kitchen in his usual cumbrous manner, colliding with corners and muttering something that was not words exactly but which was closer to words than anything else.

VI

One More Cup of Coffee

The sky beyond the window now holds the final stages of this good afternoon light ahead of imminent dusk, and every layer of the past feels right there, a touch away, the old life, and this one in its countless repetitions, today a compilation of a thousand ghosts. Michael has no yearning to move. His limbs are heavy, and the covering blankets give him a sense of being buried alive. His place beneath is a cocoon of warmth against the sting of the room's air. He draws a long deep breath of that cold, tasting the refreshment, and spends it slowly. Beside him, Caitlin smiles. Her eyes are closed and she is flirting with the notion of sleep. The smile could be for anything but he knows that it is in acknowledgement of him. She is reading the sigh, from experience, as a draught of satisfaction. Her own breath comes steady and small, unnoticed except by comparison.

A little after three o'clock. Still early, but already the day feels drained of its juices.

He settles back on the pillow and allows his muscles to slacken. After a minute or two, Caitlin stirs from her own rut and eases against him, turning her body into his. He draws the blanket up around her shoulders to protect them both from the cold.

'Like old times,' she whispers.

'Not that old,' he says, just to tease.

But talking is a mistake. Words only get in the way. Spells are brittle things; difficult to cast but easily shattered, and now that he has track of the time, sleep is no longer a viable solution. He sighs again and closes his eyes, but the darkness he finds waiting has a suffocating heft. Against him, some thought causes her smile to widen, and he feels the tiny pinch of her teeth digging in through his undershirt's cotton just above his right nipple. It's not a bite and it doesn't quite hurt, but it hints at the potential for more, and in response his hand moves, in the laziest way imaginable, down her body, over her hip bone's curve and the smooth stretch of her thigh and then slowly back up again across the corrugating jut of her ribcage. She hums playfully.

'More?' she asks, teasing.

He grunts. 'You wish.'

The place could benefit from a fresh coat of paint but, as with most pit-stop hotels, a premium is put only on the essentials. Yet the egg-white walls and ceiling, faded and rubbed as they are by the creep of time, fit well within the day. The light dictates terms here; darkness gets by in more suggestive, insinuating ways. And it is easy on the mind, something to look at and think about without having to actually care. Streaks of a shortcutting brush are clearly visible across the ceiling, especially where the daylight catches. Such things don't matter much, but details fill pictures, and Michael toys with the implication, relating this shoddiness to other things – to what he and Caitlin have together, to life with Barbara, and to himself, all facets of himself. He lets his mind run until sadness hits, then pushes such thoughts away.

Lying against his chest, Caitlin can again feel the dull drumbeat of his heart. The sensation soothes at first but then all at once begins to trouble her. She thinks of a trapped bird careening over and over into the bars of its cage. When she can bear it no longer, she pulls away and slides out into her own space in the bed. Her breathing comes in stabs as the new cold hits her, but she waits it out. The tendons of her back and limbs tighten, and when she opens her legs beneath the blanket she can feel the void that Michael has left her with. A trickle of warmth weeps from her and her pelvis shifts in some sort of impulsive retrospective gesture, but instead of recapturing the fullness of her memory it merely emphasises the sense of solitude. She shuts her eyes, keeps them closed for some time and tries as best she can to regulate the intake and the expending of her lungs. She is weary, and sleep now would be a magnificent end to things. But sleep will not come because she can't let it.

The bed sheets cling to her feet, thighs and low stomach. Her skin is still clammy and her nipples, puckered to smallness, have become hard as nutshells. Twenty years ago, even ten years ago, and with the bulk of an hour still left to them, they'd be resting to recuperate for round two, and in their minds and together running the kind of calculations that would allow them yet another shot at the title. But time changes so many things. She makes do now with stretching her limbs to their fullest extent, pleasuring in the hymn of resistance that her body sings. Even the soles of her feet ache. Ever so slowly, she is turning to stone.

'You okay?'

For a second, Michael's voice seems alien. Then it reattaches itself, or the sense of it does. He has the blankets pulled up to beneath his armpits. She knows every inch of him, by kiss and by compassion, but even after all that has been shared, he still feels embarrassed to be seen by her. She smiles, keeping as much of it as possible beneath her surface. But he fails to notice. And then she stops smiling.

'I'm just thinking,' she says.

'Thinking.'

'About us.'

'What about us?'

'I like the sound of it. The word, I mean. Us. You and me equals us.'

He laughs. It is a small, deep-set sound, utterly inoffensive, that rattles like rocks in a can. 'I like it, too,' he says. 'After all these years, finally being raised to the status of a mathematical equation. Who wouldn't like that?'

'Smart-ass. No, I'm just weighing up.'

'And here we go with the fat jokes.'

She smirks, despite her best efforts not to. 'Fine. I get it. Vaudeville awaits. Now, you done?'

'Yes, ma'am. Sorry.'

'I wasn't going to mention this yet, especially since the day up until now has been so nice, but there's something we'll need to talk about.'

'Sounds serious.'

'Well, it could be. I keep telling myself that we have time, but no one ever really knows. We'll leave here and you could be hit by a car, or I could. That's how it happens, you know. An accident, a heart attack, a bolt of lightning. The world is turning at a thousand miles an hour. Sooner or later, we all get spun loose. No one avoids it for ever, and nobody is ever prepared. And once it happens, all that remains are the things left unsaid, and the promises that can't be kept.'

Gales of wind beat at the glass but feel kept at bay for now, and in this bed, warm and safe on the edge of sleep, the stillness holds. The notion of love remains a distant but dominant focal point, hanging like Jupiter above Coney Island, a golden chink of light after several million miles' worth of emptiness and dark. Knowing that, and believing in it, is what sustains her during their time apart, particularly during those interminable nights when the borderlines of the apartment contract and the tedium turns crushing. A glint, just to capture her imagination, to lead her on and, hopefully, get her through.

Nights for her are always the worst, lying there while Thomas slumbers, cut intentionally adrift to the outermost margins of her side of the bed, not just to get away but to bask in feeling condemned, and staring, in a kind of mute rage at first but with the slog of hours in an increasingly lumpen and hypnotic stupor, at the familiar shapes

173

of the room furniture reduced to looming silhouette and at the dead-black, inch-wide crack of the wardrobe door hanging ajar and hinting at a special kind of netherworldly doom beyond.

The memory of Michael then is always within reach, his face familiar down to its planes and hollows, the slight cleft of his chin's dimple, the creases that rake his brow and nest along the corners of his steady, occasionally hawkish eyes. She likes to imagine being married to him, and wonders often about the sort of life they might live, so bound to one another. Would it still be love, would it all come apart once there was no longer the exciting shade of danger to smear the details, or would their intimacy somehow develop into something even greater? Love might be a fusion of the indecipherable and the familiar, but could the delicate balance still hold if one element were to so out-muscle the other? Such questions are a torment, especially during the small, desperate hours of night, but sometimes, isolated beneath the sheets and sweating into the pillow, she'll pleasure in this pain and even make efforts to heighten it, urging herself along with a knowing touch, into a battleground of pure feel, rubbing until the spark ignites to let her know the bristle of herself and then soon or soon enough the soft, meaty fire. She hates herself during these moments, and especially in their cooling aftermath, a hatred that is ridiculous in and of itself and yet genuine and genetically earned, the chastising haunt of good old Catholic guilt, seemingly dug out a clear couple of generations back, treated into apparent oblivion by questions and by logic, but there still like turned air along the extreme edges of life, designed to mark the divide between absolutes of bad and good and, always, to inhibit. Yet she can't stop. Sin – if that is what this is – fuels her, helps her to endure. And alongside her, blissful in his rut, Thomas sleeps the damned, dead-weight sleep of a man who has long ago found contentment in settling, and she likes to look at him in the darkness even as her body strains towards the shock of a higher state, because seeing him there, so near and so close to sharing in her deception, adds to her sense of despair, and her loneliness. Her touch quickens and sometimes she has to bite down on the edge of the quilt to keep from crying out, and all the while, even as her eyes absorb her husband's shape and character, shut-out, muscle-slumped, slightly nasal in his dreaming, her head teems with thoughts of Michael, with sense-recollections of his hands on her, his fingers, his weight against her, the bloated pounding of his body and the whistle that edges his breath as the frenzy nears for him and then explodes.

This thinking and doing represents an intense kind of cheating, not merely the fireworks and streamers of an affair but one brought right into her deceiving half of the marriage bed. And it is such a better step removed from those nights, blessedly occasional these past few years, when Thomas can't take to sleep so quickly and after twenty minutes spent boring into the latest Louis L'Amour Book of the Month Club instalment, *Under the Sweetwater Rim, Trouble Shooter, Ride the Dark Trail*, something like that, stirs and reaches out for her, his voice and words half begging, half insistent.

She bears his advances by turning away. It doesn't stop or inhibit him, but it at least spares her the ordeal of having to participate and frees her up for the running of her mind games. She lets him help her out of her underwear then, telling him to kiss only her neck and collarbone, if he must kiss her at all, and not to speak, or to do so only in whispers. And from there it is minutes more to an end, time made flesh with him wrestling against her from behind, the stubble-ridden scrub of his mouth and face furrowing into the crook of her neck, hissing muddy sounds against her ear. The reality is true enough, at least on a nerve level, but the darkness loosens facts, and in this position, stretched out on her side and facing the wall and the doorway, she can close her eyes and disconnect, so that Thomas quickly loses one identity and takes on another. There is always music playing low, soft summertime country, Merle Haggard, Willie Nelson or Tom T. Hall, and even when her husband starts to speak of love, whispering it as a boiling wetness against her skin, the night has already begun to ease and turn calm, so that his words count for nothing. Caught in that clinch, with his forearm and cupping hand tucked beneath her armpit and curled around her chest, holding her against him, her loneliness feels immense. And even when her body cries out, or even if, as tends to be more likely, it doesn't, she understands completely that, without Michael, she is alone. Not lost, exactly, because she knows where and who she is – but lonesome. The way half the world probably feels, the half who have stepped wrong and lost out on a soul connection, the half whose marriages have already sprung and are now in the sluggish, painful process of winding down. The way a god might feel, if there is indeed just one of them and not an entire Greek or Celtic plethora and if the heavens really do gape with otherwise utter emptiness. And after Thomas has finished and fallen back into the sleep of the contented and the ignorant, she is left alone to toss and turn and finally, inevitably, to ponder. The heart asks so many questions and offers such a multitude of consequences. She has sweated and shivered away countless thousands of hours chasing its promises and trying to understand their meaning and intent, she has held them in her mouth, tasting their shape and feel, and has let them run her body and soul into the sky and into the ground. And now, short of anything definitive, she has settled into a state of denial.

'Love,' she says now, considering the white hotel room around her and the dead white Coney Island sky beyond the window, 'is the story we make up to justify all the rotten things we do.'

'So cynical. And you a writer.'

'That was true, once upon a time. Or nearly true.'

She looks at Michael's profile, then looks away. Her voice, when it comes again, has fallen a notch.

'Thomas is in line for a promotion. Assistant Regional Manager for the Midwestern district.'

Michael opens his eyes, but doesn't move.

'Sounds like a big deal.'

'He thinks so. Lately, he's taken to speaking in capitals.'

'When will you know for sure?'

'A couple of weeks. A month maybe. I don't know. But he'll have to fly out for some interviews between now and then, so I'll have free days. And nights. If you're interested, I mean.'

'Is there a chance he won't get it?'

'There's a chance, but it's his turn. And it feels wrong to go wishing against him, because this is what he wants, what he's been working towards, all these years. It's just that everything is happening so fast. I'd settled, you know. In my mind. I'd really begun to believe that where I am now is where I'd always be. And I don't just mean New York, I mean my life. I made myself into the person I am. It wasn't all by choice, and I lost things along the way, but that's how it worked out. I settled. And now, Peoria. Christ, I can't even picture the place in my mind. I've seen photos, of course. When he first mentioned it, I went and looked it up. But a photo doesn't make it real for me.'

For a while, she is resolute in keeping her eyes shut. It is a trick, but her mind equates darkness with the altered perception of reality. In the shapelessness of dreams, time has no limits. Whole lives can pass in half a heartbeat and a perfect moment can somehow stretch towards for ever.

The room's stillness holds and soothes. The bed sheets are nice where she has warmed them but bitter cold even at the merest inch's remove. The material, coarse from starching, feels surprisingly good now against her skin, and she thinks about the number of lovers, both honourable and illicit and in varied combinations of age and gender, who must have come together to share this same space, these same sheets, to sweat and breathe and spill in an effort to sate their essential appetites. She imagines them, slightly repulsed by the idea of their strange bodies and slightly thrilled too, but stops short of thinking of them as people with lives as real as hers, with feelings and needs in any way the equal of her own.

When she opens up to the world again, everything has changed. The afternoon's glare has stiffened into a sullen dusk. Wanting more than anything to stay here for ever, she sits up in the bed and runs the fingers of both hands back through her unkempt mess of hair. The hour has the feel of midnight, with nowhere near that depth of dark but with the same sense of lateness, and the caution that forbids or inhibits loud talk. She discovers that she is tired and, despite everything, happy. These late afternoons are a box of contentment, worlds and lifetimes removed from her regular existence. Partly in demonstration, partly in thanks, she turns and leans on top of Michael, setting her weight both-handed against his upper chest, and kisses his mouth. Almost asleep, he is taken by surprise and for a second his breath seems to stick inside of him, but then he lifts himself to the challenge and she feels his teeth part and his tongue gently daub the flat of her own tongue. She smiles, which causes him to smile, too.

'A taste,' she says, pulling away and climbing down the mattress on her hands and knees towards the foot of the bed. 'Not a meal.' The sound of him follows her, his dozing, half-hearted protests that seem childlike because she does not get to see his face in conjunction with the voice.

Finally, the thermostat is beginning to do right by them. She can bear the room's air, if just about, and elects to dally in her nakedness, conscious of Michael's stare but pretending not to be. His attention is no longer about hunger. These days, one fall counts as a clear knockout. But she likes that he still desires to look. She eases her hair back from her shoulders and lets it spill to a midway

179

point of her back, and the simple gesture of raising her arms achieves the effect of moulding her body in the way a sculptor might, shaping everything just right, tucking and stretching, emphasising the curves and undulations. She raises her head with a kind of knowing pride, stiffens her chin, and moves to the window.

The magic of earlier, the rusted, rotten splendour of rides peeled down to skeleton husks, has been absorbed by the twilight and there is little now to be seen apart from suggested shapes. She can identify details only because she knows they are there. The world is altered by the day's dying, even though, in physical terms, nothing has actually changed. Still, she stares, past the ghost of herself growing ever more definitive in the glass, while the wind beats out the last gleam of the twilight and the minutes pass, and night comes down. And when she can see nothing more beyond her own reflection, she draws the curtains, turns and switches on the room lamp.

Immediately, Michael cries out and throws a desperate forearm across his eyes. This too is part of the game, and the light, they both know, is a gesture rather than a necessity. But today, of all days, it feels important. She wants him to be able to study and enjoy the sight of her, and to have this memory for all the years to come.

'Keep an eye on the time.'

'I don't want to go,' he says, lowering his arm and wincing against the glare of the bare light bulb. He watches her standing in profile at the foot of the bed, straightening out the undergarments that lie draped over the back of a chair, until she can no longer deny the feel of his gaze and turns, slightly and briefly, to acknowledge him.

'We need to think about moving,' she says, hating how old she sounds.

But he is not yet ready to yield.

'Come back to bed, can't you? It's still early.'

Time is a shard of glass embedded in the neck of the day. The afternoon has been as close to beautiful as any they have known together. Ageing brings certain joys, even as it tears others away. But as always at the turn of afternoon, the shadows have once more begun to deepen.

Occasionally, in certain circumstances, words get to be just words, worth their weight in sound purely for their cadences, inflections and sheer musicality, and with all meaning and truth set wilfully aside. Over the years, in such moments, they have discussed the notion of kicking free from the bullshit shackles of work, home, life and all the etcetera codicils, and just running away, flying north to set up again in some small town where there's space to be had and no one has to know them or what they've done in the name of love. Finding some idyllic little nest fit for two migrating love birds, and starting over. She's not after jewels. A bus ticket would be enough, and rental listings for apartments in Boston or swamp shacks in Louisiana. They'd get by, leaning on one another.

But if there is blame to be laid in this then it must be shared. Because talk is easy, when divorced from expectation. From early on in their relationship, they contented in the rumour of happiness, allowing their world to exist primarily in the abstract. Now only the rationed monthly afternoons are real; the rest is colour and shape

181

considered mainly from skewed angles and odd distances, and devoid of – or removed from – most if not all sensibility. What they have, and have always had, are words, false promises that nevertheless ring with the essential notes of truth. Their love is well meant, and honest, and in no way lessened by their inaction. Time has deepened the understanding each has of the other, an understanding, free of judgement, that counts want, need and desire among its blessings, as well as a knowledge of what lies within the other's heart. Fires can blaze and fires can smoulder.

Now, though, wanting is no longer in itself enough. Something is about to be broken.

'Come on. Ten minutes. That's all I'm asking.'

She stands naked, in semi-profile, on the floor at her side of the bed. For a few seconds her stare holds to some distant point, but then she looks at Michael and smiles. He holds out a hand to her, and she starts to reach for him but stops herself.

'More coffee, I think. One for the road.'

'I don't want coffee.'

'It'll heat you up.'

'You do that better than coffee can.'

She smiles again. 'Ten years ago, maybe.'

'Let's stay.' He struggles to sit up and settles for an awkward crouch, turning himself onto his supporting elbow.

'What?'

'We could,' he goes on, flushed with a sudden enthusiasm. 'The room is paid up until tomorrow. What's stopping us?'

182

'Well, let's see. How about, my husband and your wife? Your sick wife. How about those minor details, just for a start?'

He struggles again to bring himself upright. The blankets bunch around his waist. Funny, how the mind works, she thinks, as her eyes of their own accord pull away from him and seek out the room's chair, and the blue-and-white checked pattern of his boxer shorts splayed uppermost on the neatly folded stack of his clothes.

'Where there's a will, there's a way.'

She can feel him grinning without even having to look.

'Tell me about the way.'

'Better yet, come to bed and I'll show you.'

For a second, she considers putting him to the test. What he is proposing is, after all, exactly what she wants, which is for them to be able to spend the entire night together, separated from the world and its worries, free of the dictates of the clock. To be able to take their time with one another and maybe, in three or four hours or whenever the mood and the hunger overpowers them, to get up, dress and go hit the high spots, find some cosy little Spanish or Italian restaurant. Enjoy a bowl of paella or a plate of spaghetti, split a bottle of average red, all the while leaning in, rubbing knees and conversing in slow breaths, making the best and the most of the candlelight. If everything they have is to come apart, a day, a year, even centuries from now, wouldn't it be something to know that at least they've had one perfect night together, and that they spent it eating, strolling, kissing and sleeping, properly sleeping in one another's arms?

This is their chance. Tomorrow then would be molten terror, the nth degree of Hell, an ungodly maelstrom of screaming, tears and maybe – for the first time in all her married years – even a hand to the face, open or fisted but thoroughly earned. There'd be humiliation and fear, and entire histories and futures fractured and rewritten. Hearts, once they've been shattered, never fully or properly heal. But those consequences remain for now beyond the horizon because tomorrow is not today.

She lowers herself onto the bed. One leg folds beneath her, opening her body to him in a way that seems inviting until she brings her other leg up and into place. Part of the difficulty is that she knows the limits of her selfishness, and of her courage. Michael's hand settles high on her thigh but he makes no further advance, and she does not react except to lean in, only because he is close enough, and kiss his face and, very gently, his lips.

'Do you really want to stay?' she asks.

Then, without waiting for a response, she pulls back again to a sitting position. His hand tightens a quick pulse on her thigh, and his silence is answer enough. She is sensitive to every perceptible shift, no matter how minute. A tone flattened, a filament of tension creasing the brow, a stiffness infiltrating movement. The day's perfection hangs in tenuous balance, the knots waiting again to tighten. They are an argument waiting to happen, and it's better not to push the issue because after twenty or thirty minutes, once the reality sets in, she'll have to sit there and listen while he talks them back from the ledge, his voice small, his eyes in desperation, once again seeking the room's corners or the sky beyond the glass.

He wants, more than anything, to be with Caitlin, in this room, here on Coney Island. Out here, with one another, they've found the world. The air is alive, the water shines, and there is an enduring sense of shivering stars and moonlight. But even though he and Barbara have fallen decades out of love, the cancer is eating holes in her, and she's fragile. He will probably hide behind an excuse, a business call that needs making, a deal hanging in the balance or some heavyweight account about to fall to him after six intensive months of legwork, and Caitlin won't call him on the lie, because she understands. They need to consider the pain their actions will cause. It's a question of duty. Lovers, those that survive, learn to feed on scraps, to make the best of things, the best of every-thing. They lie, cheat and deceive, and they try their damnedest and more to keep the searing ache of want from tearing them limb from limb and open from belly to chin.

What this is, in essence, is cowardice, on both sides. And even when the excuse shifts a little, its colour remains the same. He'll apologise, in a way that presses beyond the blandness of sincerity, a sorry not just said but truly meant, with a kiss in lieu of flowers, of jewellery. And she'll struggle into her best and most saleable smile and let him off his impaling hook with a flippant flick of the wrist, insisting that it's fine, that it really doesn't matter. They've already done the time on this, and the motions don't change. If she lets it go that far, it'll play out the way it always does, and she can either remain beneath the sheets and quietly watch him dress or else clamber out of bed herself and turn her back on him so that they might dress together. It's not much, but it's what they have. Either way she'll talk all the while, playing the situation down, talking about almost anything else, the weather, the room, the idea she's been toying with about changing her hair. Words that seem to mean something more than their timbre would suggest, down beneath their snaps and crackles, but which keep themselves out of necessity to whispers, or perhaps to gasps, and delivered around a smile heavy with all or most of her teeth showing and that holds in place even with her back turned. A smile made big so that there can be no room to spare for tears.

The best option is to do nothing, to just let him be. This is a game that time has eroded and refined, and a slip now might prompt exactly the wrong sort of offer, one that he has neither the means nor the inclination of backing up. But at least part of why they work so well together is her ability to see all the way through him. Secrets never stand a chance between them, because they are each far too easily read. Dreams are fine in their time and space, but pragmatism is the key to survival. That, and making do. Some people see a glass as half full, others see it as half empty. But there is a third group, a small, almost unnoticeable percentage, who want nothing more than the opportunity to quench their raging thirsts. The little moaning sounds and grumbled, out-loud wishes are a part of who Michael is, was and probably ever will be, and once Caitlin learned to recognise that side of him then acceptance came so much easier. Now his hand has warmed her thigh, and suddenly something shifts inside of her and she has to resist an urge to press herself to him. He is studying her body, the sidewise sag of her

186

small breasts in this slumped position, the soft puffed bloom of her nipples reddened to puce by the falseness of the lamplight.

'Sweetheart,' he says, and now, finally, his hand comes to life, pushing like a tide forward and down into the crevice between her thighs, causing her breath to catch with a grunt. For a second their eyes meet. He is smiling, but barely. She is not, but she can feel herself yielding to the gentle press of his fingertips.

Before things can go too far, she forces herself to withdraw. And once they are apart, she turns her back, sits on the edge of the bed and cradles her face momentarily in her hands.

'Watch the time. I have to be getting back.'

Then she pulls her fingers again through her hair and gets to her feet. He doesn't protest, which reveals his advance as another empty promise. And because of all that could be coming, because there is a falling number now attached to each such day as this, turning precious every touch and whisper, she feels her throat begin to constrict, the way it does when tears are close and trying not to fall.

Making the coffee is a precise repetition of the earlier process, yet something seems off. She attributes this to the fact of the lamplight and how it changes so completely the atmosphere of a room, and it is only as the kettle hushes towards a boil that she realises the difference has to do with her state of undress.

When it feels safe to do so, she glances at Michael and grins. He is watching her, but his mind seems elsewhere. The blankets are bunched at his waist now, showing off his full undershirt-clad girth. Seeing this arouses pity in her, not as a thought but as something almost physical. She can feel it turning over in the bottom of her stomach. Pity and, again, the certain dread that all of this, what they have going, is running towards its end.

'Did I tell you how beautiful you look today?'

He means it, but she lowers her eyes and laughs.

'That's easy enough to say when you're lying in bed without any shorts on and I'm standing here naked in front of you.'

He shakes his head, no, but doesn't need to bother with the word.

The kettle nudges towards boiling point, giving her an excuse to turn away. She knows what he has in mind to say and is thankful that he elects silence instead. Because she is too close to giving in. She busies herself with the coffee, out of necessity reusing the earlier cups, partially filling them with boiled water, swirling the water to remove the dregs and then tossing the mess into the empty white ceramic basin that sits perched on the far right edge of the dressing table. But even after she wipes out their innards with a wad of tissue, the cups retain a certain murk, the greyness of old newspapers. They have little or no weight to them, and turn translucent when held against any light. At home, in an environment where cleanliness approaches a clinically sterile state, she'd never tolerate anything as shabby or as off-putting as these. But here, she gets to feel differently. Here, dirt and its kind feels rather fitting.

She adds a sachet of coffee to each cup, then pours in the boiling water and stirs. The ritual acts as a kind of capping point, a summation. Coffee to say hello, coffee to say goodbye, or goodnight. She adds sugar, and carries the cups, rattling as before on their saucers, across the room to the bed.

'Michael.'

Michael has, in the interim, closed his eyes. Her voice see-saws the name, which startles him awake. Actually, it startles her, too. She rarely speaks his name, or at least not his full name. She rarely needs to. In conversation there is no reason to do so, although he does enjoy calling her Caitie and she rather enjoys hearing it, especially during moments of intimacy. There is something gorgeous then about the way he says it, whispers it, as if it is a fact that she absolutely needs to know but for whatever reason does not, as if the shapely spike and drop of her own truncated name holds the only answers she will ever need.

'What? Oh, yes.'

He sits up and takes the coffee from her, muttering thanks. She crawls back into bed, rearranges the pillows behind her and settles the blankets over her stomach. She leaves her breasts exposed. They are small but shapely still, splayed now by the posture of her body. Once she is comfortable, Michael passes her a cup, and for a while they sip in silence.

Even with the addition of sugar, the coffee tastes terrible. That lesson was there to be learned first time around but it seems that neither one of them was ready for the education. Instead of fusing, the sugar's sweetness exists in a weird tandem with the bitterness of the coffee. She steals a look at Michael and sees that he is sipping too, in a dainty fashion, with the saucer held beneath his chin and the cup tipping in a set rhythm to his lips and away again, over and over. A kind of pale intensity has set itself into the flesh of his face.

From month to month, their routine barely deviates, yet a lot has changed over the course of their time together. Ageing has something to do with it, and not just in a physical respect. They are no longer the people they were back when their lives first collided. They have evolved, slowly, to where they are now, and to who they are, each massively influencing the other's growth. Love causes people to consider themselves from more than one vantage point, and encourages them to become better than they are. Sometimes that is an attainable goal; most of the time, it's not. But even trying counts for something. And even if, at the core, nothing does actually change, a new kind of consciousness at least comes into play, one that shadows every act, every decision taken or not taken. People in love, or in what they might in their own delusional state consider to be love, tend to live their lives with others rather than themselves in mind. And that makes all the difference.

In more ways than not, they are a better fit for one another now than when they'd first met. The way a favourite old sweater always wins over a new garment in terms of pure comfort. As much as anything, this is the gift that time has given them, the illusion of comfort. There is a preciousness in being able to open up to someone, in being able to say aloud the kind of things – dreams, dreads and longings – that it never seemed possible to share or discuss with anyone else. Between most people, a kind of fear exists. Love lies in getting past that fear to the open space beyond. Once that happens, failure is no longer important. But no one gets there easily.

Today has been a good day, better than many they've known. Often, the mood is just wrong, or one or the other of them is too tired, or too knotted with tension, or simply too elsewhere. Half a dozen times at least during the past two years, and less frequently though still occasionally over the past decade, their efforts at lovemaking have fallen flat. Age contributes to that too, though it is not wholly responsible. The first few times it happened, Michael's reaction was to shut down. He couldn't look at her, could barely bring himself to speak. She understood, and said so, rubbing his neck and telling him not to worry, assuring him that these things happened once in a while. But he'd gone beyond listening. Tension passes between people, the way electricity does. There is much more to the world than what the five senses catch; there are also vibrations.

Time's truest gifts to them have been a tempering of guilt, a sharing of blame, and above all else a deeper understanding of who they are as individuals, and as a couple. Acceptance has become their mantra. Realising these things allows them to breathe in one another's company, to not be afraid of saying the wrong words at the wrong time, and to be able to cope whenever the engine stutters and breaks down. Over time, they've come to understand that there are all sorts of ways of making love, and all sorts of love worth making. And even on the down days, neither one of them has ever seen the hours spent together as time wasted. They have learned to value the little things, the quirks and foibles, because it's the

191

flaws that most thoroughly differentiate one person from the next, the otherwise hidden peculiarities that make intimacy such a treat. Like the tiny freckle on the lobe of Caitlin's left ear, just where a piercing would be, a kind of *x marks the spot*. It is a nothing detail, and is unlikely ever to trouble the classification of beauty, yet it becomes beautiful somehow, because it is hers and a part of her, a sweet little speck of a thing hauling focus to itself time and again during conversation and during the act of love. Or the way she snorts when something catches her just right and causes her to laugh too hard, the sound of it small and cute, just some up-breath reflex action of her tongue falling wrongly against her palate, leaving her help-less against its coming through. These are the aspects of a person that can't be affected, just as Michael's peculiar fascination with order and the straightness of lines and angles can't be, or the problem he has with odd numbers, as exemplified by the way he can never stop mid-book on an uneven page and how, twice a day, at lunchtime and again last thing at night, driven by some illogical terror of imbalance, he has to empty out and count the loose change in his pocket. In his desk drawer at work, and tucked away in the locker beside his bed, he keeps small glass jelly jars full of hoarded pennies and nickels, a secret stash that he has spoken of only with Caitlin, and which he refers to, for her amusement, as his bank vault. Such blemishes and oddities are precious, because they keep away notions of dreaded perfection but also because they help to make each a little more real in the other's mind. Time has given them this, and because of time's revelations even something as simple as a cup of coffee has value for them now, even a bad cup, in a way that it could not possibly have had back when they were younger and in need of greater thrills.

Caitlin drinks her coffee, propped up against some pillows and with her shoulder set against Michael's arm. Everything feels magnified, including emotions, and it will take very little now to make her cry. A word about loss, a look of sadness in Michael's eyes. He drinks from his cup in long pulls, despite the heat. He has abandoned the saucer onto his lap, which frees up his right hand. For a minute or more it lies at his side, then it reaches out and settles awkwardly, palm-outwards against her stomach, just above her navel. Seconds later, it slips beneath the blanket's hem and nestles into place at her crotch. He doesn't look at her but gazes straight ahead, and she does not look at him but concentrates on keeping her breath even and on finishing what is in her cup. She moves only once, almost imperceptibly shifting her hips to resettle herself against his touch. He parts her legs but only barely, and his hand continues to move, an inch up, an inch back down, over and over, slowly, in a kind of hypnosis. This too, comes with time's passing, this level of knowledge.

She kisses his shoulder and collarbone, presses her face to his neck. He removes his hand only to relieve them both of their cups, then closes his eyes and takes her mouth against his own. 'I'm yours,' she tells him, simply, as if it is nothing but the truth. He tells her that he loves her and she nods and says that she knows, which she does. He turns in to her and this time, freed of burden, his left hand moves for her. It moves slowly and, again, settles, and this time it is perfect in its place and full of under-standing in its touch. But this is a coda, shutting things down for now, in nice, pleasant fashion. And with nothing more ambitious about it than that, it can be fully enjoyed, for exactly what it is. Tasting the bitterness of the coffee on his tongue, she lets her own hand roam and explore. Even as pieces change, even as details bloat or sink, thicken or turn to mud, there is a comfort to be had in their familiarity.

'I love you, Caitie,' he says again, as if it is a thing that constantly needs repeating, and she smiles against his mouth in acknowledgement and nods a thank-you even without breaking from him. 'I love you too,' she says, and she twists her body for him, sets her left leg between both of his, raises it until there is nowhere left for it to go and gives utterly and completely of herself, to be taken into his embrace.

VII
Icebergs

Having brought the bad news home with them, Barbara had spent her first hour back in the house drifting in and out of rooms, moving like long grass in a strong breeze, with all the soundless grace of a dance. At first, Michael followed along behind, holding far enough back so as not to encroach but stubbornly filling the spaces she'd vacated, ready to catch her should she fall. She kept laying her hands on surfaces or picking up small objects to hold for just a moment before setting them down again, back in their rightful place, but their details hardly registered.

Noon lay smothered in rain. A cold heavy fur of mist muted everything, weather made for whispers. At every window, the dim light seemed to penetrate her body. It was clear that Michael had missed a lot of the signs. And in this light, everything blurred, the way it does when tears come. But he was not yet ready to cry.

Once she'd worked through the downstairs rooms, she slipped out into the hallway and pulled the door shut behind her so that he could not follow. She hadn't spoken a word since their return, but the closing of the door was a clear statement. In the living room, he held his breath and listened as her slow footsteps carried up the stairs. He could feel himself beginning to break. So much needed saying but the words would not come. Even in his mind, they refused any semblance of order.

Within a minute, she was overhead, her heels like finger-snaps on their bedroom's laminated floor, loping to the world's slowest waltz. Then a radio came on, Sinatra as a murmur, with a melody he'd always loved: 'The Way You Look Tonight'. The dancing stopped, and he knew that she was sitting on the edge of their bed. He stared at the living room's shut door and, in his mind, could see her, perched on a corner of the mattress, stooped forward, elbows digging into knees. All angles, transfixed by dread.

The specialist had said that weight loss should have been an indication of something awry. A thick-featured, slightly piggish man, with flesh the pulpy, fat-freckled paleness of raw sausage and eyebrows like spools of copper wire. He'd shaved carelessly and had nicked the flesh of his upper lip just above his mouth's left corner. When Michael cleared his throat and muttered that Barbara had always been slim and that there'd been so little excess weight to lose, the man's eyes hardened and held to Michael's for a heartbeat at least longer than was comfortable. He could have gone on and explained that, with Barb, right from the very beginning, changes had never been obvious, that apart from a certain piecemeal tightening of the skin around her eyes and mouth, her body remained much as it had been when she'd first unfurled herself for him all those years before. But the doctor's stare held, until it became clear to them all that this was about needing somebody to blame.

They'd expected something like this. Doctors had prepared them, in an offhand sort of way, with particular phrases dropped in passing during the straggle of tests and scans. But even with the worst in mind, the sheer finality of the confirmation still threw them headlong into this state of matching shock. A punch in the mouth still hurts, whether you see it coming or not.

When she reappeared, evening had already fallen. She stood in the kitchen's doorway with the hall to her back, reduced to silhouette by the rancid amber cast of the street's sodium lamp. Michael, perched against the red slate counter and buried in his own thoughts, didn't realise she was even there until some minute disturbance caused the room's equilibrium to shift. He looked up, stunned at how much of the day he'd lost. Full darkness had fallen. And outside, the rain was still coming down.

'Hi.'

She nodded, from somewhere else. 'Yes.'

Forgetting it had lain before him for hours, he lifted the cup that he'd been hunched over and sipped some coffee. It washed cold and rancid over his teeth and tongue. But, rather than spit it out, he held it in his mouth, then swallowed.

'Did you sleep?'

She shrugged. 'I'm not sure. I dreamed, but I can't say for certain that there was sleep involved. Christ, Michael, how can I hope to deal with this?'

'You will. We will.'

Her hand reached for the switch. In a violent instant, the light flared and with a small popping sound was lost, and for several seconds a searing afterglow bled through into their vision, giving the darkness a more pervasive heft. That instant of the light, though, had chiselled for him a shocking image of her face, pallid, elongated, with her hair tousled and askew and her mouth slack with awe.

Now, even beneath the weight of darkness, all the cracks lay fully exposed. He drew a quivering breath.

'Can we talk about this?'

'Can we, or will we?'

'I'm serious, Barb. I really think—'

'What good will talking do? Apart from putting a bit of noise into the air.'

She stepped from the doorway into the kitchen, and vanished, and there was a moment when the world fell, softened to perfect stillness. The rain, which had been whispering against the window, pressed tightly to the glass and lost its sound. Everything felt caught between beats, and Michael wondered if this might be how death would feel, this same sort of deep-tissue inertia. But then a sob broke the surface, a dislocated thing but vital, and enough to return some semblance of balance to the night.

'Sometimes, the things that break us apart seem less if we keep them hidden. If we talked now, what could we say that'd be any good?' Her voice, disembodied in the blackness, felt new and strange.

'It's okay to be afraid. Cancer is frightening.'

'There are worse things than being afraid, Michael. There's being alone.'

'Don't say that.'

'Why not?'

'Because you're not alone.'

'Bullshit. I've been alone for years. We both have. That's who we are. That's what we are.'

He wanted to argue, but hadn't the strength. 'We need to eat,' he said, his voice low because of the darkness. 'Should I make us something, or would you prefer to go out?'

'Out. Of course. Always out.' Because silence in a public place could be far more easily masked.

Without discussion, they decided on Chinese. Something about the bulk and heat of that cuisine appealed, especially tonight, something about the physical aspect of the food, the portioned variety of the bowls, the textures, the colours. And Chinese to them always meant Wong's, a snug lamplit eight-table restaurant on the East Side, the area's best-kept secret. Rarely ever more than half full, Wong's liked to prioritise taste and quality of product above all else. They'd discovered the place quite by accident, some ten or twelve years earlier. Michael had been recommended a then-new Lebanese restaurant on the same block, but the night of their cold-call coincided with a birthday or an anniversary party and the noise and revelry sent them reeling back out into the street, unfed and unfulfilled. It was a decent break, one of the few in their married life, and it quickly became their place, whenever they felt in need of a night out.

Tonight, even though they hadn't called ahead to reserve a table, Mrs Wong stood waiting to greet them on entry. A small, fat-bodied woman in her late sixties or seventies, she lowered her eyes, curtsied and let Michael take her hand, then turned, her face lighting up with love and worry, and embraced Barbara, the way dear friends do. Wishing them repeated welcome, she led the way to a table near the back, theirs by favour and habit, and once they'd settled, began pouring tiny slender welcoming glassfuls of a pale plum liquor. Ten minutes later, she came back through from the kitchen with a platter of shredded-duck spring rolls, simple fired shrimp, jiaozi dumplings and a ginger soy dipping sauce.

The decor, which belied the splendour of the food, was basic, the walls around them kept to an unobtrusive lily-white shade that reflected the subtle lamplight and kept the focus on the few traditional two- and three-colour prints, delicate empty-space paintings of vague mountain peaks, low-hanging cloud islands and intruding trees, skeletal apart from the small pink hearts of blossom and contorted for the sake of balance.

They ate in a distracted way, their attention mostly fixed on the few other diners, their minds open to the occasional draughts of caught conversation. Two middle-aged men in suits sat at a table near the fireplace wall, doing more drinking than eating, and over by the large blinded window, a young mixed-race family. As Barbara watched, the family erupted in bleats of shared laughter. The man was American, probably mid-twenties, with a very serious expression except when he laughed; the woman, slightly younger, Chinese and pretty, with dark eyes and shining black waist-length hair draped over her shoulder in a single woven rope of ponytail; and two small children, a boy and a girl of about an age with one another. As a unit, they looked mismatched, yet perfect. The man set down his chopsticks every few bites in order to hold his wife's hand or even to kiss her, in a most gentle and adoring way. And with every kiss, the children, who could not have been more than four or five, the boy with a short heavy bowl of hair fringed low above his eyes and the girl with her hair long like her mother and in braids, squealed and made teasing sounds of happiness. Being kissed in so public a manner embarrassed the woman, but it also evidently thrilled her, and after parting she bowed her head shyly for a few seconds in an effort to conceal her smile.

Michael considered them in a vague way, then focused on the shrimp. Barb, though, continued to watch. Something about witnessing the kiss caused her eyes to narrow and grow small.

'I always assumed I'd see old age,' she murmured. 'Funny how we delude ourselves.'

'So. You're giving up, is that it?'

Her expression was stone, possessed of a hardness that told its story in cracks. Her shoulders hitched, then fell.

'Call it that if you must call it something. Anyway, maybe it's for the best.'

'What is?'

'Well, you must admit, it does simplify things.'

He glared at her. She felt it, but didn't bother to meet his eyes. She'd seen enough of him, and this other family seemed much more interesting.

Across the room, the little girl climbed down from her chair, stood beside her father and began an adorable recitation of 'Puff, the Magic Dragon', her voice demure, with a sweet, brittle lilt. Feeling some sense of duty, the two men in suits stopped drinking so that they could give the show their fullest attention, and Mrs Wong came through again from the kitchen. The soft way that the girl pronounced her R's lent the song an added poignancy. When she slowed into the final notes, everyone applauded, and one of the men in suits pinched forefinger and thumb into his mouth to the first knuckle and whistled in a long, shrill catcall. Blushing hard, the girl slipped back into her place at the table, but the applause went on and at her mother's urging she stood again and issued a quick, reluctant bow.

'Cute as a puppy,' Barbara declared. 'Isn't she just the sweetest thing?'

Michael lifted the last of the dumplings and sank it into the ginger soy. He ate it in three bites, taking his time. Barb picked at the remnants of a spring roll that she'd torn open, fishing out morsels of meat and shredded vegetables with a kind of surgical precision, her chopsticks clacking like a reprisal of the just-dead applause.

'What do you mean, "It simplifies things"?'

She looked up. Her lips were clenched shut but her front teeth worked a sliver of duck.

'It doesn't matter. Forget it.'

'It does matter. Come on, Barb. If you have something to say, then say it.'

'Why? So that we can get it all out in the open? No, thanks. I feel bad enough about myself already. Let's just eat, okay?'

They ordered. Michael opted for skewers of beef with a special spicy satay marinade, and a side of jasmine rice. Barbara, after professing a vague interest in something fishy, let herself be guided by Mrs Wong and ended up with king prawns in a deliciously light sweet chilli sauce. A basket of steamed dumplings arrived unordered, compliments of the house, a selection of oyster, chicken and vegetable. Michael asked for beer, even though he had no particular appetite for drinking. Barb took another glass of the plum liqueur. The food tasted wonderful, but there was too much of everything.

'No one is talking about an end, Barb. You need to get your mind right. I understand that you're afraid, but you do yourself no good by jumping to conclusions. It's serious. Of course it is. All cancer is serious. But nobody has mentioned terminal, have they? If that was the prognosis then they wouldn't even bother with treatment. We have to take the positives from that.'

Barb chewed slowly, resignation making glass of her eyes. And her voice, when it came, was soft and empty, almost contrite.

'Sounds nice,' she said. 'But you don't believe it, so why expect me to? I know how these things work. We both do. We've been down this road before, and I recognise the scenery. And doctors always tell the best side of the story.'

He shook his head. 'That was a long time ago, and a different situation.'

'You heard what they said.'

'What? That the treatment will be fairly intensive?'

'Invasive was the word they used. And there's no fairly about it.'

'Intensive, invasive. At least they're doing it. And I also heard them say that they're hopeful of a positive outcome.'

'Or they'll start carving.'

'They said it might be necessary to consider surgery. But that's only might, and it's not today or tomorrow. They'll give the chemotherapy a chance first. That'll break it down to a manageable size. I know how it sounds, and anyone would be terrified, hearing it, but the news could have been a lot worse. So try to have a little faith.'

'What does "hopeful" mean, anyway? It's a nothing word, really. When you think about it. Hopes are much the same as wishes. We don't get to decide whether they come true or not.'

Barb took another bite and smiled.

'Forty-eight isn't really much of an age. Not any more. In parts of Africa, maybe, but not here. These days, it's barely the halfway line. And plenty have had it worse than me. A lot worse. And yet, I feel old, and I've been feeling old a long, long time. Remember when we first started going together? We couldn't keep apart. And you were as bad as I was. Worse, even. After we bought the car, you used to drive down from Maine or New Hampshire or wherever you were selling, clean through the night sometimes, just so we could have breakfast in bed together. That was love. Or so I thought at the time. Why did we stop doing things like that?'

Despite everything, even with the insinuation of the cancer, she looked good. She might, as she said, have felt old, but age, at least so far, had barely touched her features.

In a certain light she could still have passed for thirty, possibly even younger. But she was right on an essential fact; whatever it was that once lay between them had long since faded.

Michael asked for another beer. Barb thought about taking a third drink but decided against it. Mrs Wong came to the table and poured the beer, then emptied the bottle's remainder into an unused wine glass. Simple problems have simple solutions, she said, showing little yellowish pebbles of teeth and resting a hand lightly on Barbara's shoulder. As usual, and as expected, taking sides. Widowed since before they'd known her, she was a simple sort of woman, old-fashioned and stoic in her manner, used to enduring. Though Barb only ever addressed her as Mrs Wong, they'd developed quite a friendship, particularly over the past two or three years, and the old woman had been to their house on more than a few occasions, as an invited guest for dinner or Sunday lunch, sometimes accompanied by her son and daughter-in-law but, more often, on her own. Now, she held the empty beer bottle by its neck and stared openly at Michael before walking away.

He drank the beer, and Barb gazed at a point some inches left of and above his shoulder. Then abruptly she reached for the other glass. Spumes of froth feathered her upper lip. She daubed at it with her tongue, then wiped herself clean with the heel of one hand.

'If it's any consolation,' he added, 'I feel pretty old myself tonight.'

The family across the room had almost finished their food, and now the children were growing restless, particularly the little boy. He kept slipping from his chair onto the floor and then clambering back up to the table. The boy's father, serious and serene, made no attempt at chastisement. Instead, he turned, reached out for his wife's little eggshell chin, lifted her face to an angle and kissed her again. She said something in response, quietly, the words hidden only until the music broke.

'Jimmy, please. People are looking.'

'So what?' the husband, Jimmy, answered. 'Let them look. Let them see what love looks like.'

Playfully, she pushed him away. He leaned back from her, smiling, and raised both hands in a gesture of surrender. Then the music came again, light piano, hums of violin, the same or similar to what had already gone before.

'Sweet kids,' Barb said, half in a whisper. 'Kids like that would keep anyone young.'

Michael finished his beer, and counted some notes out onto the table from a small roll of fives and tens, more than enough to cover their meal, the drinks and the gratuity. Very suddenly, he'd had enough.

'Say I die.'

'No.'

She came out of the en-suite bathroom, wearing just a butter-coloured bra and a pair of cerise-pink silk pyjama bottoms. He stepped out of his pants and folded them carefully into their pleats.

'No. I mean, speaking hypothetically, let's say I do.'

'I know what you mean, and I mean no. I don't want to do this.'

She stood watching him from her side of the bed. His clothes were building a neat stack on the seat of the Canterbury that had been with them almost from the beginning of their married life, a good piece that they'd stumbled across in a Dobbs Ferry antique store while enjoying a long weekend up in Westchester, and bought as a restoration project for Barbara, who at that time was looking to take up a new hobby. Eventually, because an amateur hand could achieve only so much before real expertise was called for, the Canterbury ran them some significant cash, probably double the chair's most generous valuation estimate, but the quality and age of the piece warranted the investment, and they'd never had cause to regret the outlay.

'Well, has it occurred to you that maybe I want to do it? That maybe I need to? You're involved. I know. But think about me, for once. Is that asking too much?'

'I am thinking about you. It's cancer, Barb, but you're not going to die. So don't torment yourself.'

She unsnapped her bra. Her breasts slipped from the cotton cups, medium-sized and slightly elongated, bottom-heavy but still firm, still shapely for a woman of her age. Her nipples, in the lamplight, lay like muddy thumbprints against her pale flesh. Michael stared, but didn't react.

'You know, there was a time when you'd have capsized this bed to get at me. We were insatiable then. You'd come in from work and some nights we wouldn't even make it through dinner.'

'I remember,' he said, grinning for her sake. 'Call it the impetuosity of youth. Before the bastards ground me down.'

There'd been no break in the rain. Over the past hour, a wind had risen, and it beat now in flaps against the side of the house. It was weather to match their mood, yet the room was comfortable and warm, the soft lighting holding the worst of the night at bay. Michael picked open his shirt, folded it with the same attention he'd given his pants, and sat into bed. But because exhaustion and sleep were not mutually exclusive, he switched on the radio, keeping the volume low. Music had a way of deterring talk, or at least letting them feel easier about saying nothing.

On her own side of the bed, Barbara had slipped into the top piece of her pyjamas before becoming distracted by some thought or memory, and the buttons remained undone. Her face was empty as she reached for her hairbrush. Michael watched, feeling the measured cadence of the strokes that she pulled through her hair. The brushing was a ritual, and strictly unnecessary. Even in a tousled state, her bob, full to neck-length, kept its easy style. When she leaned leftward, one lapel of her top eased away from the swell of her breast and revealed her body again to him. She had become thin. He could see her ribcage in clear lines and, beneath her throat, the channel behind the prominent ridge of her clavicle. Even before she'd finished with the brush, he sat up, set the alarm clock, then lay back down and closed his eyes. It wasn't about sleep, it was about escape.

She cleared her throat in a soft way. 'I might read. I'm not sure that I'll be able to concentrate but it might help to take my mind off things.'

He opened his eyes, then closed them again without looking at her. 'Fine.'

'You're tired. Won't I be disturbing you?'

'It's fine. I probably won't get to sleep anyway.'

The bones of his body were leaden, but his mind had again begun to churn. He knew the signs. Insomnia had marred his recent weeks and months. He drew a deep breath and waited.

After a minute or two, he felt her climb into bed beside him. Their bodies didn't touch, but a balance shifted. He had to struggle for calm.

She kept a small, frequently replenished pile of magazines on her bedside locker, and she reached for one now and began to amble through the pages. He listened, as he did with the rain and the music, trying to let the whispers of the paper wash over him. Even an hour of sleep would be something. Gradually, though, curiosity set in, and he began to wonder if her particular magazine selection could be identified simply by the sheer weight in sound of the pages turning. He found himself picturing the various copies: the short yellow-trimmed squatness of the *National Geographic*; the airy loose-leaved swagger of *Rolling Stone*; *Esquire*, thickset and stylish but, even without wrong-stepping, not really her bag at all; the *New Yorker*, pitching indulgence and sophistication, in an ironic way far more her thing. He listened for clues, but all he heard was the slick rustle of paper, shuffling along at a rate which indicated that she was settling mostly for the pictures, maybe reading the captions but not much else.

And then, eventually, she gave up trying and returned the magazines to her locker.

He waited, with not quite bated breath, for the snap of the bedside lamp's switch and the plunge into a deeper darkness. But nothing changed. For long seconds there was only the noise of the rain and wind outside, and in the room, the murmur of Springsteen, low but audible on the radio, singing an old song, 'Stolen Car'.

'Are we finished?' she asked, at last. Taking him by surprise.

'What?'

'As people, I mean. Is this all there is for us?'

The answer was no, of course no, but suddenly it felt like such a difficult thing to say and actually mean. So he said nothing.

'I still dream about him.'

He opened his eyes but resisted the urge to move. His body was a dead weight, trapping him.

'That's natural. Don't worry about it.'

He cleared his throat, which helped, but only a little. The bones of her shoulders and hips could be felt through the material of her pyjamas. He knew her angles by heart even without having to reach out a hand, though a part of him suddenly ached to, just to connect again in some small way.

She turned her head and gazed at him. 'It doesn't feel natural.'

'Of course it is. He's part of your life. That won't change.'

'Do you think about him?'

'I don't have to. He's there.'

'Tell me.'

'Barb.'

'Please, Mike. I need to hear. I need to know that it's not just me.'

210

Michael sighed. 'At first, he was in my mind all the time. I could think about nothing else. But the world has only a limited tolerance for grief. The first year or two, he was everywhere. So I did what a lot of people do – I threw myself into my work. I cried twice a day. Honestly. It became routine. I'd feel the tears coming on and would go and lock myself in a toilet cubicle. I learned to weep in a silent way. Trial and error, but I got there. Sometimes I'd catch people watching me after I had returned to my desk, but no one ever said a word. And gradually the tears came less and less, and eventually they stopped falling altogether. But I haven't forgotten him, I've never forgotten. He's still with me, and there's not a day goes by that I don't miss him.'

The space gaped between them, oppressive with insinuation. Michael wondered if she could feel it too, or if time for her had simply brought acceptance. He was unprepared for how much pain he felt at the realisation that, were he to reach out for her now, she was as likely to pull away as she was to turn in to his embrace. Or that, worse still, she'd simply lie there and bear him. Because who had given up on whom in all of this? What had always seemed so clear now felt anything but.

Her smile in profile had a wretched shape to it, turning her haggard.

'When I dream of him,' she whispered, 'he is nothing like I remember. Sometimes he's a boy, sometimes a teenager. Occasionally he is a man, fully grown. It only happens a few times a year, and there's never any kind of order or pattern to it. But it doesn't seem to matter because I always know it's him. He might look different, but he hasn't changed at all. They're just dreams, but I don't know, they feel so real that it's like I'm glimpsing some alternate reality. I can smell the salt and vinegar of his skin, I can hear his laughter and his breathing, always making his words a little heavy, as if he's been running. He talks, but I never think to ask him the questions I want answered. I think I'm just happy to listen. Sometimes, his hair is thick and a little wild, and when I touch his arm or shoulder his body feels as strong and hard as a tree. In the dreams, it's almost as if I'm the ghost, I'm the one who has died or faded away. I know it's ridiculous, but I often wonder if what I see goes beyond dreams.'

Michael counted breaths, not yet trusting himself to speak. He thought about the unseen pieces that made up the world, the insects in the forests, the chemical elements of the air, the mountains of rock shifting and boiling tens and hundreds of miles beneath the surface. And set deep down in his chest, his own heart beating life throughout his body. All necessary links in a chain, all existing, but on a level beyond observation.

'Does he seem okay?'

'What?'

'In the dreams. Does he seem okay? Does he look happy?'

She bit at her lower lip. The idea that he might have been anything other than happy had not occurred to her.

'I think so. Yes, I think so.'

Every inhalation felt suddenly precious. He often thought about this, and had come to understand it as a question of awareness. Each detail held its own singular importance, yet also lent support to everything else.

Scientists put the rate of death at two people every second of every day. And, at the same rate, four new lives began. Universal connectedness was a comforting thought, but the greater truth seemed to be that every soul spun through its days and nights alone. Watching the victims of famine or war on television, witnessing their screams and mutilations, their sad-eyed, fly-bitten faces, bellies like gourds swollen to bursting point, made him want to weep, yet within minutes or an hour he'd find himself laughing about something innocuous. Even though it was human nature to want to care, people really only truly noticed one another in moments of collision. Love was real, but a delicate flower in need of constant nurturing. It bloomed for a while in brilliant ways, but too easily wilted.

If this were to be his final breath, would he even know? Would the end announce itself, or prefer to work in secrecy so as to prevent panic until the last possible moment? Thinking about this, he tried to focus on the breath in his mouth, but the idea arrived too late for due consideration and he found himself too suddenly out of air. An instant later, a tide of new breath poured through him, but any relief he felt was tempered by the understanding that, whether recognised or not, this would be how the end would some day come. He decided that, given a choice, he'd rather the flank hit than an advance warning.

'And you're certain it's him?'

'Of course I am. I know my own child, Michael. It's him.'

'Good,' he sighed, not wanting to fight. 'That's something, at least.'

The radio worked as filler. No longer Springsteen now but something of the era. Leisurely piano, plunking raindrop arpeggios and a nice thumbing bass, perfect for the lateness of the hour, the notes sullen but calm with a knowledge of grief, or at least an understanding of loss. And in time a scratched voice, Bob Seger, pent up, battle worn.

'Do you think there can be anything to it?' Barbara asked. She'd begun to cry.

Michael shrugged uselessly. 'Who can say? There are things we understand and things we don't.'

'I'm losing my mind. Sometimes my thoughts run wild. But talking about them is too much.'

The tears traced a stripe of wetness to her ear. As he watched, they bristled among her lashes, then spilt again. Until he moved, he didn't know what he was going to do. He turned to her and drew her into his arms. Far from resisting, she pulled herself against him, with desperation and something like terror in her grip.

'No, it's not,' he told her, in a tone that he might have used on a child, but speaking it first against her cheek and then the corner of her mouth. 'Talk yourself hoarse if it helps. We all need to make the best of things, Barb.'

Every good piece of the past felt near, and for these few minutes they were young again, other people, or other versions of themselves, with all the old need between them. Her lashes feathered the skin just beneath his eye and her tears soaked and softened his lips. He recognised this as a transient moment, ships in the night, but there were times when that in itself could be enough. And later, after she'd finally drifted into sleep, the top of her pyjamas still unbuttoned and spread wide, her bottoms bunched somewhere at the foot of the bed, he smoothed the tangles that their exertions had put into her hair and kissed her face again, her cheeks and then her mouth and chin, and when he kissed her eyes, their rapid dream movements shifted and flickered behind their lids, as if stimulated to respond. But she was asleep, and he was wide awake. He brought the duvet up over her chest and shoulders. Her breath whispered thinly through her nose, making the barest sound. He watched and listened, then eased away from her, slipped from the bed and without even glancing back pulled shut the bedroom door and went downstairs, to make coffee, to watch some rerun ball game or an old movie with the sound blocked nearly all the way out. And as he stood in the kitchen, waiting for the coffee to percolate, the image that filled his mind was of how fresh her unconscious self had looked, lying there eyes-shut in the lamplight, and how beautiful. Sleep had managed to turn a trick with time, but only one shard of time. Somehow, at a point in their embrace, and as if mortality's brink really did become her, she'd regressed to her fullest flowering, to the time of their marriage's earliest days. And in that same moment, he'd been dragged in the opposite direction, and plunged into a state of decrepit old age. Young hearts sleep, old ones sit up watching the darkness, and waiting. Long past midnight, alone at the kitchen counter, the truth of their lives turned pale and then dissipated, until it became difficult to tell who, exactly, was dying and who was cursed to keep on living.

VIII

Goodbye, My Coney Island Baby

Michael faces the door to dress, Caitlin favours the window. The electric light emphasises the day's recession. Without it, the hotel room would be lost in almost total darkness. First to finish, Caitlin begins to resettle the bed. Michael stands aside to let her pass, and watches without comment while she smooths creases from the blanket. She works as if alone, then straightens up and pulls a rope of fringe from her eyes. She seems to want to smile, but cannot. These are always among the loneliest moments of their month. Michael, feeling the need to, smiles for both of them. The expression pleats his brow and the bridge of his nose. He reaches for her, only because she happens to be so close, and grips her lightly just above her elbow. She steps against him and yields briefly to his mouth. Then her hand flattens in the dead centre of his chest, not pushing but setting a kind of boundary. Because they have already passed the point of this.

They part, and Michael fastens his overcoat and holds the door open. She steps out into the hallway and waits, eyes averted, while he surveys the room one final time to assure himself that they are not leaving anything of themselves behind. This is something he always does, and part of it is habit, the fear of a mistake. But there is also an element of preservation in the act, some need to burn the details into his mind, just as it is, empty but alive still with the feel of them, the scene of their latest crime. Then he switches off the light, and they go.

At the station, the train is at the platform. Everything about Coney Island looks different in the darkness, especially when considered through the sleety curls of a north wind. The place exudes a menace that is absent or held to a discretionary distance during daylight. Alleyways yawn, horned music seeps through walls and locked doors out into the early night, full of diminished chords and open ninths, already swinging every kind of wrong.

They arrive in good time, a little out of breath. The cold has intensified with the night, and the air has become thick, scalding to the lungs, infiltrating anything that has not been bound up tight. A hundred steps out of the hotel, Michael's hip began to ache, and in the ten or fifteen minutes it takes for them to reach the station, a pronounced limp has him bobbing leftward, every step tipping him repeatedly apart from Caitlin. To compensate, she takes his hand.

218

The threat of snow is undeniable now. A blizzard has been forecast. Michael has known the island snow-clad and with the inherent misery of a bleak north wind at fullest blow, the boardwalk layered in sludge, the footpaths treacherous even to a careful step. But wanting the small comfort of a contrasting image, he envisages instead a morning left bright and idyllically still, with a perished sun stuck in one corner of an otherwise empty sky and everything else caught in deepest slumber, the whole scene, pier and Ferris wheel, streets and ocean, cloaked and flattened in shades of shining white. It's a dream, a fairytale, but tonight, in this cold darkness, dreams are what he needs.

The old man at the hotel desk had not even glanced at them as they left. Bald and grey-skinned, with a long face narrowing over a square chin and heavy black-framed glasses perched high up on a thin Roman nose, he sat forward, leaning on one elbow in a way that set him lopsided, and as they approached and came abreast of him he kept his attention fixed on his newspaper. Michael, bothered by this and even a little bit angered, had wanted to stop and draw the man's attention, to force some acknowledgement for what he'd just condoned under his or his boss's roof. But Caitlin's determined step had urged them ahead, and after they'd passed the desk it ceased to matter quite so much. They strode on through the small lobby, side by side and of a pace with one another but keeping modestly apart, the staccato gunshots of their shoe heels sounding steady and if anything too assured on the faded mosaic floor tiles. A table stood against the wall just left of the doorway, with a small white-and-pink marble top, the bisected remains of something originally octagonal but now trapezoidal and two-legged, its otherwise impossible balance assured by a hidden fix. Perched in the centre was a narrow blue ceramic vase with a pair of nylon daffodils protruding from its fluted neck and facing away from one another, and scattered on the marble, like fanned blackjack hands, two randomly tossed sets of room keys. That hotels like this still exist, ones which specialise primarily in short-term stays, is down to economy and demand, and they shape their service accordingly, operating this kind of convenient drop-off system, and accepting, and indeed actively encouraging, straightforward cash transactions. As they skirted the table, Michael lifted their own keys from his coat pocket and set them down, with discretion, alongside the others. He was easy with it, having done this sort of thing before. But he still knew better than to look back.

At this hour, just coming on for six, the station should be crowded. During the summer months the platforms will be dense with bodies, with kids laughing, music of ten different genres banging new decibel levels into the already straining din. Shorts and shirts, shoulder bags and boom-boxes, the smells of sweat and salt and fried food. But this is wintertime, after dark. There are some people about, a couple of dozen or so scattered throughout the building, but each is bent against the cold and stiff with his or her own intent, their minds already elsewhere, at home, at work, in the arms or the bed of a loved one.

Michael leads Caitlin out along the platform to the train. Despite the imminence of their parting, and all that has been said and aired, a certain satisfaction is evident in their movements. They look properly coupled, as though they belong together, each completely considerate of the other's needs. When they reach the doorway of the middle carriage, he steps aside and with a small gesture invites her to board first.

'Where do you want to sit?'

Behind her, he shrugs. 'You decide. Anywhere is fine.'

She takes a few paces forward, far enough from the door to shield them from any draught, and slips into the window seat of a twin berth on the aisle's left side. The walk has left them dishevelled. Even though they kept to the shelter of the buildings, the wind, pocked with random flurries of hail, was a blade. Now, warming slowly in these seats, it takes a moment to relax. Michael's left hand falls to his thigh and he begins to knead at the flesh, trying to loosen the ache from his muscle. When Caitlin catches his eye, he smiles wearily.

'Getting old.'

'Yes. And grey, and full of sleep. But the tune is still sweet.'

He nods. 'Sometimes. When I can play it.'

This is the beginning of the end. They have a little time left, but have already started drawing back from one another. There's trauma in this, nourished by guilt and self-loathing, but also a tinge of relief. Lovers for years, but time has left its marks, and they've learned to rely on their mechanisms of defence. It's a process, this inward retreat; bracing for another month to come, another month in exile. The problem is that an eruption is imminent. There should be more days like today still ahead of them, but there's also a strong likelihood, when she leaves this train, that this will be a full-blown goodbye. They won't admit it, but that dread has become one of the colours of the night.

In an hour she'll be at home, and daydreaming her way towards bedtime, filling the last of the evening with dinner, steak maybe, and a few greens, depending on what's left in the freezer. And potatoes, if Thomas insists, though he probably won't. According to experts, once you touch a certain age you must be conscious of what you eat. And mantra is the key. Repeat a thing often enough and you'll begin to believe it; believe it long enough and maybe you'll even start to heed its warning. And these days, potatoes are, pretty much, the devil. White bread, too. Thomas has been trying to cut back on the carbohydrates. He keeps insisting that he's not a kid any more, hanging the statement out there as if in hope of contradiction. Steak is still, for now, an option, but in restaurants he has taken to ordering the fish, something he never used to do. Talking up things like turbot and flounder, forking the air with his enthusiasm, insisting that she try a bite, just to taste, because the body takes such an age to break down beef. It's possible that he'll ask where she's been all day, but it won't be meant as an interrogation. And he'll accept whatever she says, because it suits him to do so. She'll busy herself with putting on water for coffee or buttering a piece of bread, any small chore that keeps her moving and from having to look him in the eye as she answers. She has learned that airy distraction equates to innocence. It's all to do with tone. So, today, she'll say, was about lunch with a couple of the girls. Nothing too exciting. A birthday celebration for one of her invented friends, Harriet, or Lucia. The name she chooses will be new to him, but he'll still try, with silence, to conceal this fact. Just in case it's someone she'll expect him to know.

She'll tell him that they chose a nice place, too; a little bistro in the Village, maybe. Just a salad day, though, apart from a slice of cheesecake. But it was a birthday, after all, and a soul needs its nourishment. They stayed on, chatting and drinking coffee until nearly three, and the place was empty when they left, but of course nobody said anything. And the rest of the afternoon got lost on book shopping. It's always the same. You go in with one thing in mind and then get distracted at a cost of hours. Today, in the Strand, it was the Anne Tyler shelf, and a new translation of early Neruda poems. That'll be enough, because books are the one subject guaranteed to tune him right out. But, should something more be required, she can easily bracket the excuse with a few shoe-store visits, detailing some hopeless search for a pair that might go close to matching her newest dress, the off-white with the gold and green leaf. Really, it's all about telling him what he expects to hear, and what will be easiest for him to believe.

A ghost watches her. The glass at her left shoulder is crusted with dirt. The soluble whiteness of the carriage's lights burn an overlay against the outer dark and, inches away but set somehow deeper than that, caught in the fold between dimensions, her reflection has an eerie hollowness, there but with a textural suggestion of absence, like a memory of someone already departed. Everything is shadows and light, the way the whole world is, every image made up of one and the other. The face gazing back in black-eyed stare looks both like her as she is and has always been but also like she'll perhaps be, some twenty, thirty years from now. Some elements align with what she knows by heart, but at least as many jar. Exposure to the wind

223

has savaged her. She makes a spirited but futile pass at patting down the corkscrews and flapping spools of her hair and, tired to the bone, leans her head back against the seat's rest and closes her eyes. When she opens them again a second or two later, the ghost is still watching, expressionless and full of judgement. She faces front, trying to escape, then lowers her gaze to the fumbling game her fingers are playing above the wedged crevice of her lap.

The train door shuts, a shuddering action that shifts the equilibrium. Michael looks at her and nods his head, almost as if she has asked a question. Stupidly, she nods in response, and sets her hand on the back of his. They sit there, braced for something, but the engine comes alive from a place within, a kraken stirring. Caitlin feels the vibrations rise up through her, full beats of time in advance of any sound. And then they are easing forward. So much goes unseen, so much exists beyond what the brain can definitively comprehend. Movement, atmosphere, love.

'Are you working tomorrow?'

His teeth clench, making something mean of the sigh. 'Oh, Christ, work.'

She looks at him. 'What?'

'Nothing. Don't worry about it. Just the usual bullshit.'

'I thought things were going well for you.'

'They are. For the most part. At least on a scale of nickels and dimes. But a lot has changed. These days, I nearly have to get down on my knees and beg just to get what should be mine by rights. There was a time, not so long ago either, when a handshake meant something, you know? When a man's word was diamond. Now you close a deal and ten minutes later you find out the punk kid at the next desk was listening in on your conversation the entire time and that while you were on a toilet break or dropping off some mail for the afternoon collection he had the balls to punch redial on your phone – not his, mind; yours – and settle for a commission slash just to undercut and undermine you. And you know what they say to that when you take the matter upstairs? Initiative. Good for the company. They don't care about decency, or honesty, or honour. They don't give a shit. If they can save half a cent on a job, they're ecstatic. Money is the thing now. Nothing else matters.'

'You could pack it in.'

'Right.'

'You could.'

'And start afresh?'

'Why not?'

'At my age.'

'At our age.'

Someone has decorated the carriage's ceiling, overhead and all the way to the far door, with great explosions of graffiti. A whole woven nest of shapes and lines, done out in a spaghetti of luminous colours, gaudy as a Daliesque depiction of Hell and as impossible to ignore. The colours of dreams, maybe the colours of screams. Michael doesn't even try to decipher what he is seeing. Graffiti is one of the newer art forms, less an act of vandalism than a method of expression. He decides that he can accept it, and far more easily than, for example, bullshit like the Readymades, largely because graffiti has to do with the creation rather than the creator. And decipherable or not, there is, from a purely aesthetic consideration, a crude beauty to what has been done here.

She turns his hand over and their fingers entwine. The skin of his palm is cool and dry, stiff against the softness of her own. She loves holding onto him, especially in public places. Usually this causes him anxiety but tonight he is either too tired or too content to care.

'Barb's cancer is a complication.' He gazes past her at his own reflection in the glass. The added distance makes his mirror image vague, frail yet somehow all the more disturbing for that. The bones in pale relief, the gaping pits for eyes. He wants to look away but is transfixed. 'But maybe it simplifies things, too.'

'Don't, Michael. Don't talk like that. And please don't put it on me.'

'No. I'm sorry. My mind is running, that's all.'

Outside, there is nothing to be seen. Darkness engulfs the world. Scuds of sleet hit the glass and leave little scars behind, slash marks that cause tiny dissections of the night. Caitlin's reflection, a part of all that darkness and yet separate from it too, as if existing on a different plane, watches with a lost expression.

Holding back from the thoughts she doesn't want to face, she turns her attention instead to the few other passengers, five in all, spread throughout the carriage. A young Latino couple who have positioned themselves across the aisle from Michael and two seats forward, as well as two women and a man, each travelling alone.

This is an old game, made for artists and spies. Everyone a character waiting to be written, if she could ever manage to bring herself back to the page, everyone a potential hero. A few rows ahead, on the aisle side of the seat away from the window, is a tall black woman in a black suede coat, with dreadlocked hair pulled back into a tight ponytail that emphasises her leanness, and her beauty. Large silver hoop earrings and the collar of a brilliant scarlet blouse, dark full profiled lips whenever she turns her head towards the glass showing pinkness just where they meet, and huge dark eyes threatening the gamut from ferocious to succulent. Next, across the way, is a white woman, probably Irish but certainly some genus of Celt, middle-aged, overweight in that bulging, thick-bodied way that some women get when they have mothered well and often and some get by straightforward genetic inheritance, layered in cardigans and coats, with large round rose-framed glasses and, absurdly, a yolk-yellow baby's bonnet hat with what, from these feet of distance, looks like a mottled pattern of green and blue flowers. White ribbon bindings hang undone, straddling her engorged cheeks like tears that have turned to ice or fused into bone. And finally, beyond and on the same side, close to the front of the carriage, a young man, stone-edged Baltic and sickle thin. Wearing his dark hair tight at the sides, full on top and neatly combed out of a left parting, with meticulously shaped sideburns that angle nearly all the way to the corners of his mouth. He sits sideways in his seat with one leg thrust out into the aisle, his slim booted foot bobbing in mid-air, and sucks on a thinly rolled cigarette even though smoking on the train is forbidden both by the red-and-white wall sign and by the law of common sense. Again and again, he gazes back over the arm that rests along the seat's upper frame, as if expecting the scene in that direction to somehow change, his eyes bouncing from face to face in screaming dread of finding someone he might know.

A fine cast, full of potential, different in every surface way, yet sharing an isolation.

The couple are something else. They are in love. Perhaps as young as sixteen, certainly not yet twenty, they talk in whispers and sighs, full in their contact with one another and restless only because that is nowhere near enough for them. Caitlin can only see the back of the boy's head, with its crow-black hair cropped nearly to his scalp, and the narrowness of his shoulders tucked inside a white-collared shirt and fraying denim jacket. Entirely the wrong sort of clothes for the weather, but at that age, and that much in thrall, boys do not feel the cold. The girl he's with has the window seat and so Caitlin can see her face clearly, and it is a beautiful face, the skin tawny in the searing whiteness of the carriage's strip lighting, probably a little darker in the natural wash of day. Her large black eyes simper, dreamily hooded, and her full, pouting mouth veers in little snaps between the coyness of a grin and a condition that is serious to the point of brusque. In stillness she looks her age, a late teen, but in talk, even in unheard talk, the movement turns her terrifyingly young. Her front teeth are large and childish, each critically separate from the next. That is probably one of the things about her that the boy finds most captivating, a morsel of detail on which to focus, and one that comes easily to mind for him during the smallest hours of lonely nights. As part of a different face, those teeth could compromise the fine balance of attraction, but for this girl they are just right. Her hair, rich and full of her ancestry's Indian inkiness and gleaming with the captured magic of early night-time, is worn long and tossed, carelessly youthful, and kept from her face by a simple red plastic band. From word to word her face widens and contracts, the talk like breath, urgent and essential to her existence. Elongated, heartened, stretching, slackening. Yet her beauty goes unchallenged, a clear absolute set apart from anything purely physical.

The pair exude happiness. Age does not enter into the equation. Love is love, to be taken wherever it is found. Caitlin watches them until they kiss, until the girl tilts her head into just the right inviting slant and the boy, reading the situation perfectly and perhaps even anticipating it, even instigating it with a particular promise or sworn oath, leans in. Then it is time to look away, to leave them with what they have found in one another. The rest can be easily enough imagined.

'What do you mean when you talk about starting afresh?'

'I can't make it much more straightforward than that, Mike. What's confusing you?'

'But are you serious? I mean, is that what you really want? Or is it just what you think you should be saying, knowing that I'll be the one to back away?'

His hand is still pressing into the muscle of his left thigh, and she is startled to see that he has stopped wearing his wedding ring, and astonished that she didn't notice earlier. Without it, his hand and fingers look clean, pipelines of bone webbed in greyish skin. There's not even a mark where the ring should be.

'Let's stop talking about this,' she says, bowing her head.

But there is an edge of hardness in his voice. 'We can't, though. The tide is coming in. You'll drown in Peoria. We both know it.'

'And you're the lifeguard, is that it? Well, I guess I'll just have to take my chances, since you're so busy saving someone else.'

He starts to say something, catches himself and draws and spends a long whispering breath. Then he closes his eyes.

'She's dying.'

'Stop. I told you, I don't want that, and I don't want to talk about it. It's not my fault.'

'I'm not saying it's your fault. It's nobody's fault. But it's a fact.'

'They're treating her.'

'It's largely palliative. The doctor as much as told me.'

'You're not God, Mike. You can't know. Miracles happen every day. Not water into wine and walking on open seas. Real ones. Ones that count. I've read that, during the time of Jesus, the population of the whole world amounted to a little over two hundred million people. Now, in this country alone, we're heading for double that number. In the world we're talking seven billion plus change. A couple of thousand years ago, miracles stood out. But today, how would anyone even be able to keep track? They happen so often now that we've even stopped calling them miracles, but that's what they are. People are constantly climbing down from their crosses. The rate is still probably one in a million, but if you think about it, those aren't such bad odds. So, stop, okay? And don't mention it to me again.'

She is, once more, close to tears. When she glances at him, she finds his face open with concern for her, wanting only good things, and to be presented with some way of providing them. He's almost an old man, in facts if not in actual numbers, and yet he is, just now, childlike too, and grief-stricken. In the past, feeling one another's need, they'd have taken turns professing the depth of their love. But it's become unnecessary.

Up ahead, the overweight woman has decided to tie her bonnet. She has fat hands, with short but nimble fingers that taper to points, and she plucks at the strands of ribbon in a dainty, practised way, tying a neat bow and measuring the legs and loops by feel towards some acceptable balance. A small gold ring with a colourless stone adorns her left pinkie. Embedded in so much flesh, its delicacy seems absurd, yet even from a distance it is striking, and undeniably pretty.

Back when she still wrote, such details seemed often to rise up from the world for Caitlin, begging to be explored, and to be allowed to develop and even fester, with patience and good fortune, into a story. She continues to notice but, because that part of her life feels done, no longer looks so closely. But this, now, catches her eye, and again, just this once, she lets her mind run.

Ring and hand are clearly mismatched. Did the woman herself put it there? Caitlin imagines her, the bonnet lady, saving up, determined for once in her life to indulge this want, stockpiling dimes and quarters over a span of months, perhaps even years, building and counting stacks of coins at the kitchen table, during all those late hours when sleep can't or will not come for dreaming. And when the right number hits, dressing up in her best garb and visiting a store or even several stores, selecting this particular ring from a wide range of what falls within her budget, knowing by instinct precisely what she wants and searching without compromise until she is satisfied. Maybe. Or perhaps it had been a gift, the doing of a parent, some elderly mother or father producing it as a token of love from a little burgundy velvet clasp box on the morning of some special birthday or Christmas. Both possibilities feel likely, but in a story there'd be a third card to turn: the thrilling chance that the ring might possibly be the keepsake of a lover, a man who could, without flinching, look beneath the rheum of fat to where the real attraction lies. This is an intriguing thought, stunning in its hopefulness, the notion that no one is as solitary as they might seem, that there is always somebody somewhere who knows you and, more importantly, who wants to know you. Somebody for whom the rest of the world is an addendum.

The bonnet lady's chewed nails had been painted an ivy green at some point, but only traces of that colour now remain. Caitlin can see the woman in mid-polish, leaning into the milky pool of a bedside lamp and working the little brush with intense concentration, her whelk of a tongue pinched between her teeth, the green polish gleaming iridescent in wetness but finally crusting over into something definitively bland. As an act it straddles a borderline between pathetic and sweet, the tiny ill-conceived gesture towards beauty. And yet, there is something heroic at play here, something that awakens a painful innocence.

Considered in such terms, the ring really could have been a lover's gift. Certainly, there is some deep sentiment attached, as evidenced by the sheer determination of its wearing. Love and maybe only love could be the viable motivation for keeping on from the peak of those high, hopeful moments to the straight ruin of this cold day. Love, or the promise of love, a whisper of it, to keep her reaching towards beauty, to justify all that time spent striving to please or to at least sate some illusive inner aesthetic.

'I don't want you to go. I can't lose you. I'll bear anything except that.'

'I'm sorry, Mike.'

'You don't have to be sorry. Nothing is finished yet.'

'I think it is. Time has beaten us. When we were young, we still had it in us to run, but we were afraid of everything. That's life. When you're struggling to keep everything upright, the sky is always thunder, and we're constantly hunched against the next downpour. Perspective, and a recognition of what's really important, only comes with age. And by then, it's too late.'

'No, it's not. It doesn't have to be. Look at yourself. You're not even fifty, for Christ's sake. At least let us die before you have us buried.'

She smiles, but it is a picture of sadness.

'I've needed this, you know? In my life. I can't even tell you how much it's mattered. What you've given me, and what we've given each other, has kept me from turning to stone. To feel that I've been loved, that I am worth something in the mind of somebody else – that's been my miracle. I don't want to lose you either, Mike. I need you. But Barbara needs you more. Especially now.'

'What are you saying?'

'I don't know. I think I'm saying goodbye.'

'Please, Caitie. Not yet. Not until we have to. There'll be another day for us. We'll make another day. Call me tomorrow. Forget work, forget everything. That way, if it has to end, we'll finish things properly. But please, if I ever meant a thing to you, call. Promise me that you will.'

Ahead and across the aisle, the young couple really begin to go at it. The girl is transfixed by something far deeper than the carriage's ceiling. She has her big dark eyes half-lidded and her dishevelled mouth hangs open, the tip of her tongue curling out from one corner. Maybe she has heaven in her sights. And the boy, against her, kissing and licking her neck and the lobe of her ear, makes the sound of a dog lapping at a bowl of water. One hand has burrowed inside her blouse. After a minute or two, either in response to his mouth, his hand, or a combination of both, the girl produces an oddly tactile humming that seems to live somewhere between her nose and the back of her throat, a noise that is nearly tribal, or primal. It is hardly suitable behaviour for the train, but Caitlin is in no way offended. Because they are so young, they can get away with this. As long as they keep their clothes on.

'I'm the one to blame. I should have done the right thing a long time ago.'

'It's not always easy to tell right from wrong.'

'No. But we're not too late. Barb will die or she'll live. I'm not essential to the equation.'

'What do you mean?'

'Go home. And don't think about it. Don't think about anything. But call me tomorrow.'

At the next stop, the bonnet lady gets off and more people board. Three here; then, at the next station, five; and then more. The line is getting busy. Caitlin considers each of them as they enter and fill the seats, but something has switched itself off inside of her and she no longer pays close attention. These people are real enough, but somehow without essence. Yet their intrusion has tipped a balance in the carriage's intimacy. Even the young couple seem to sense this, because they stop fondling and sit upright again, waiting with a patience which runs hard against their age to get to wherever it is that they need to be.

Michael closes his eyes and keeps them closed. In this state he carries the full clout of his years; still, creased, greying all over and all the way through. Turning ever so slowly to dust.

Caitlin links her arm inside of his. She has death in mind. An end is coming, and she is frightened at the thought of letting go. At her touch, he opens his eyes but doesn't move, and in profile he looks stiff and put-upon, and she knows that he is thinking about many things at once, about them as a couple, where they are going, where they have been, about the swinging compass points of Barbara's cancer, about work, things left undone and building like walls around him. She presses her mouth to his shoulder and whispers his name, tasting the fabric of his clothes as a sweetness within her swallow, the wiry filaments of the clipped wool, the succulent dampness where the evening's sleet has caught and dissolved. *Michael.* Needing it said, needing to feel the shape of it still.

Parting now is the biggest mistake. He is close to a decision, but the hours of night, the silence and the things he'll have to see, will wear him down again, and allow his old fears to dictate. It doesn't have to be this way, of course; they are on a train, and they have choices. They can get off at the next stop, pick a direction and start

235

running. Or they can stay aboard, and keep riding until the train runs out of track. The key is to keep moving. Make do with pocket cash until they can get to a bank, stick a pin in a map and just go, heedless of the consequences, until they've found a new sky under which to live. Just as Pete, her stepfather, probably did, all those years earlier. It all feels so suddenly possible that she almost says it aloud, and maybe it is only the taste of his clothes in her mouth that keeps her quiet.

With the moment of their separation imminent, another five minutes, give or take, there's nothing for it but to accept what's been won or lost, and to settle. As gently as she can, she takes her hand back, releasing him. Again, he half-turns, and she is sure that, in his eyes, she glimpses the notion of a kiss. But either he hesitates or she does, and if the chance was there at all then it is quickly gone. Which, she decides, is probably for the best, though she knows that she'll regret missing it. Any kiss now, without adding further to the chaos, can only be a kiss goodbye.

His hand has stopped kneading, and lies crumpled against his thigh. There is something almost birdlike about it, the way the bones live so close to the surface, the way they shift in little twitches as if to a pulse beneath his papery skin. Her heart fills all at once with pity, because no one understands him the way she does, and nobody else will ever care to look so close. The smallest shift in his expression transforms him, a residue of his past making the surface and echoing some deep-seated insecurity. She has seen this before, often, and though its impact is almost always fleeting, the plaintive quality of it never fails to move her. His eyes become a compilation of small sadnesses. That he is entirely unaware of it is something that catches her just right and one of the main details of him that she'll miss to the point of tears if he really is to slip from her life.

'I'll call,' she says, giving in. 'Don't worry. I won't forget.'

'Thanks. Try to make it the morning, though, if you can. Because in the afternoon I need to be at the hospital.'

'What for?'

'They're putting a line in. I don't want to go, but it wouldn't be right for me not to be there. No one is saying so, but I think it's kind of a big deal. With doctors you learn to look for the shadows around the words. They're calling it a line. Barb is being put under for it, so it's surgery, really. I don't have the exact details other than that it'll be used for administering pain relief. Morphine. She'll be out for an hour or two, at least. But I also have some ends that need tying at the office, so I'm looking at an early start. I'll be in from seven, until lunchtime.'

'Fine. I'll do my best.'

She is annoyed at feeling hurt, and hopes that she's kept it out of her voice. Because it's not really his fault. What gets her isn't so much that he should have a life beyond her bounds but that he should be so able in managing it. Yet she also knows that his apparent efficiency comes at a high price, based as it is on a willingness to compromise. Far from an ideal, these past several years have made do with limited happiness, a life that breathes largely for its Coney Island trysts, the reinvigorating frolics that keep him upright. Every kiss is so honed by a month's worth of anticipation that the weeks between feel like dead radio air. It amounts to a cluttered existence – the pitching, selling and constant hustle of a thankless job; home's muted plainness, and the long night-time hours shared with a woman who feels more and more a stranger to him with every passing day. All so much flotsam to be navigated. Even the cancer has this sense of detail, a terrible thing for what it is, but Caitlin knows that other men in Michael's shoes would run, they'd pack a bag and get out, and they'd never ever look back. The definition of courage isn't always clear.

Still a minute or more out of the station, he shifts in the seat beside her, grips a handrail and hauls himself to his feet. Even though he remains within reach, she feels a chasm open. From her place at the window, she looks up at him. He returns her gaze, uncertain, then nods his head.

'We'll talk tomorrow,' he says, in a tone meant to reassure. Then, almost as an afterthought, he clears his throat and tells her, lowly, that he loves her.

These words are her nourishment. Even in their airing, she aches for them. She has heard him speak the sentiment a thousand times, has had the words in small-talk jabs on piers and street corners, in hushed sincerity over candlelit tables, and in whispers with his teeth bared hard against her ear as they clung sweating to one another in some strange bed. Its impact never fails to split her open, and yet it also never feels enough.

'I love you,' nearly but not quite a whisper, and the truth is to be had from the sound of his voice, the dry rustle of it. Shyness, sincerity, fear, reassurance. And, until now, commitment, all the commitment he could give and all that she could afford to take. Even with her heart punching heavy combinations in her chest and up into the small of her throat, aching to believe, she can feel in him a desperate urge to look away, just to see who in the carriage might have overheard, who might be watching. As ever, afraid. And such words are hard for him, and even at the five- or ten-thousandth time of saying, need to be wrenched loose. He wants to look away, but doesn't, because doing so will lessen everything, and they can't afford that, not now, not at the moment of their parting.

In the end, it is she who cuts him loose. She smiles, the merest turning of her mouth. And that is enough. She stops short of returning the phrase. Said one way, it has resonance. Returned, it often frails to smoke.

He lets her smile suffice for both of them, and when she turns back again to the window to watch for his stop, he lets his gaze go there, too. The tunnel is soothing darkness torn open only by the occasional amber streak of a wall lamp, but her reflection in the glass, still spectral but now more thoroughly defined by the contrasts of outer dark and the carriage's bleached fluorescent light, perches with them as a thing tethered, an accompanying second. This Caitlin, one step removed, teases like a shape from a dream, fully herself, her expression captivating in its familiarity, morsels of detail bringing the likeness alive. Even in rendered state, he can't comprehend how any man could look and look away, having missed her wonder.

And then, like dawn sifting the horizon, the tunnel lightens and the train slows and eases into the station where he must get off. The image of the second her vanishes or is overtaken, consumed, by the world beyond. And outside, there is only the platform, cold, blanched flashes of concrete and ceramic, scrubbed down and innately squalid.

He stands there, drooping like a flower after a bruising of rain, one hand clenching and relaxing against the back of the seat he has just vacated. She knows that a part of him is terrified at the possibility of missing his stop, the same part of him that is always on the edge of fear over something. There is nobody in the aisle to obstruct his departure, though even if he did somehow fail to make the platform it would be no great chore to simply continue on to the next station and then take another train back. But this is who he is. The days shared with her are, truly, a step outside himself. After a lifetime spent humbled by numbers, his instincts have become smothered. Fear drives him now, penning him into easily quantifiable constraints.

'Go,' she says, but still he hesitates.

They are sharing desolation. She opens her mouth to add something else, but falls short. Seeming to understand, he leans in and presses her with a kiss. It's what she wants, but feels so much less, the barest thing. His mouth finds hers in the most perfunctory of ways, with a kiss that commits no sin or crime, that commits to nothing. The farewell is no more profound than the greeting.

'I told you. You'll miss your stop. Go.'

He straightens up, nods his head stiffly, and disembarks.

Less than a minute later, he reappears, outside on the platform, eight or ten feet away. With the seconds they have left, he simply stands, peering through the carriage window at her. A group of people, in drifting past, have to part in order to overtake him, but he doesn't even register their presence. In isolation, he looks the way a man made newly homeless might. His coat hangs unbuttoned from his frame, and all his strength has been sucked away by the growing lateness of the hour. A ridge of his hair bristles back along the right side of his head, either from the snugness of the pillow, the pull of the Coney Island wind or from her raking fingers. His eyes are small and hard, fixated, and his face sags with all that has been lost.

Beyond the glass, he now has become the ghost. Caitlin waves, but he only returns a stare, as if he has lost the ability to move, as if the capture has been that complete. But just as the doors of the train hush closed again, the spell slips a little and he raises his fingers to his lips. When he lowers his hand, he attempts a grin, maybe so that she'll get to remember him well, or perhaps think him, in some small way, brave. But the subway's smutted air tastes hard, and the result looks pained.

Then, all at once, the train stirs and begins to crawl ahead. She rises from her seat and presses herself palms flat to the glass, attempting to stretch the moment. As she is drawn forward and away, she can see that he is saying something. Not shouting, but calling out. She watches the shift of his mouth, trying to make some sense of its silent shaping, but it is already too late. Not caring now about the tears that have begun to fall, or who on the train or the platform might see, she stands and waves a hard and broken-hearted goodbye.

Acknowledgements

This novel had a long, slow gestation, and I would be remiss if I didn't acknowledge those who helped coax it into being.

Firstly, my editor, Robin Robertson, for seeing in this novel what I most dearly hoped was there, and for taking a chance on me when no one else wanted to know. Robin, and also Monique Corless, Jane Kirby, Sam Coates and all the wonderful staff at Jonathan Cape and Vintage, helped knock it into the shape of a book, and set it loose on the world, with an enthusiasm and attention to detail that has overwhelmed me.

It feels right to remember my good friend Andy Godsell, sadly now long departed, but a poet of considerable promise and potential. Many years ago, we started out together on the long and winding writing path, and he still feels connected to everything I write.

In the years of drafting this book, more of them than I care to count, I have to acknowledge my friends, Pete Duffy, Martin McCarthy, Brian Whelan, the Julianos,

Pawel Huelle, Antonia Lloyd-Jones, Shoko Kanenari, Emilio Bonome, Emma Turnbull, Luo Xue Wei, Julia and the lovely Schwaninger family, for the support, texts, feedback and chat, and for telling me what I needed to hear, even when I knew it wasn't yet entirely true.

I am grateful also, to the O'Halloran, Murphy and O'Callaghan families, for the continued support and interest in my writing.

I owe deep and dearest thanks to John and Janet Banville. One August evening, while reading in Kinsale, my low ebb caught the sunlight, and when the greats praise your short stories the song carries weight. Their kindness is a gift I'll treasure always.

Ying Tai Chang showed up in a lot of these pages. She is half the soul of this story, and probably the better half.

And finally, my family, who live my writing with me. Martin, Kate, and the two best things that have ever happened to us, Liam and Ellen; Jazz, Yann, and my best friend, Irene – my pillars, confidantes, and most trusted supporters; and my parents, Liam and Regina. Nobody could hope to know two more nurturing, giving, good-hearted people.